Owmapow Rides Again

Stories

KJ Hannah Greenberg

Fomite
Burlington, VT

ISBN-13: 978-1-953236-60-9
Library of Congress Control Number: requested

Fomite
58 Peru Street
Burlington, VT 05401
www.fomitepress.com

12-20-21

Contents

Preface

Dr. Owen Brownstone, aka Owmapow, is a good-hearted fellow, a biology professor, a rescuer of oceanic fauna, a devoted brother, a teacher of science writing, and a wannabe fictioneer. Unfortunately, he is also an individual who is almost always disadvantaged by the courses of action in which he or his associates engage.

Nonetheless, part of what makes him endearing is his tenacity. He repeatedly attempts to embrace activities that he deems correct, no matter the number and nature of deterrents that he encounters. Despite that innate courage, Owmapow repeatedly blunders. He remains befuddled by sundry ineptitudes, i.e., remains a contemporary Sad Sack, a relatively inconsequential person who constantly confronts absurdities, even humiliations.

As such, Owmapow is all of us. He is our doggedness. He is our recurring, unexpected misfortunes. He is our bumbling. For every moment that we have felt frustrated by the caprices of empowered others or by the fickleness of Providence, we have been Dr. Owen Brownstone.

KJ Hannah Greenberg
Jerusalem 2021

Beloved Little Sister

Jan. 4, 1986
Rachel:

You will never read these words, but I am writing them down, in any case. I can't talk to you since you're little and I can't talk to Mom and Dad since they love you more.

I'm not even sure they love me. When they took us out for ice cream to celebrate your "A" in math, they said nothing about the fact that I got an "A," too.

Love,
Owen

****

Jan. 11, 1986
Rachel:

I wonder if it matters to Mom and Dad that I keep making honor roll. You get paid for every "A" or "B." I don't. Yet, I have to pay our parents when I get a "C." I only gets Cs in gym.

Meanwhile, I'm considering trying out for our middle school chess club. I'm not as good a Frank Mills or as Janet Che, but since Dad used to play chess as a boy, maybe, if I join, he'll love me.

Love,
Owen

****

Jan. 30, 1986
Rachel:

Life is so unfair! Mom spent an entire twenty dollars on skirts for you and refused to give me a measly five to update my aquarium.

I'd run away but leaving home looks bad on college applications. Just two more years of middle school and four years of high school and I can flee! I can fledge!

In the interim, maybe, I can make money tutoring.

Love,
Owen

****

Feb. 15, 1986
Rachel:

Frank says I'm a lousy chess player, but when he came over to visit, he loved, and I mean loved, my aquarium. He also said his older brother needs help with algebra and that a whiz kid like me, who is also his friend, should get first crack at tutoring his brother. Frank's going to ask his parents to hire me.

Frank's one of the only people who knows that I mastered algebra and geometry. I won't tell Mom and Dad. I'm afraid they'd punish me if I scored less than 99+ on the next standardized test if they found out.

Anyway, Frank's brother is scary. When I was visiting Frank, I walked past his brother's room. I saw a poster of a blond lady in a tiny bathing suit on his wall. I can't believe his parents let him own or display it. He's also the only 9th grader on the high school varsity wrestling team and he's in the 190 pound class! He's huge!

Well, even if I don't tutor him, Frank, who's getting tired of his pet turtle, said he'd trade that sweet reptile to me for my Don Mattingly Donruss Rookie Card. I hope that's okay since I'd be getting a live creature and he'd just be getting a piece of cardboard.

Love,
Owen

****

Feb. 22, 1986
Rachel:

Sometimes, I wish you were a sneaky sibling. If you read my diary, my life wouldn't feel so lonely. On the other hand, if you read it, then you'd know my secrets and that wouldn't work out too well, either.

In the end, I'm not going to tutor Frank's brother. His parents were nice and Frank was happy, but his brother is a monster. That kid would rather talk to me about sports and girls than about equations, functions, real numbers, inequalities, exponents, polynomials, or radical and rational expressions.

Frank and I made the trade, though. He had a funny look on his face after taking my card and handing me his turtle. I hope our deal doesn't count as my cheating him. I try to be objectively good.

What's more, his parents paid me even though I didn't teach his brother a thing. On the way home, I used most of that money to buy a container and meal worms for my new critter. I wish you weren't so squeamish—the turtle's nice to hold. So afar, he doesn't even have moss or slime growing on his back.

Love,
Owen

****

Mar. 3, 1986
Rachel:

Today, Janet Che called me a "nitwit." She cornered me after lunch and told me that the whole school knows that I'm willing to trade baseball cards for any creepy crawlies caught in cesspools, ponds, and so on.

I think she likes me. Usually, no one talks to me before, during, or after lunch. Maybe, she wants to be my friend. I know that she's a better chess player than me, that she's good at math, and that she gets high marks in Language Arts and Social Sciences, too.

Do you think she's jealous of my growing wildlife park? Since all this started, I've traded my two of boxes of baseball cards plus a handful of the cards, which I think might have been Dad's, that I found in the attic.

Despite my successful commerce, though, none of my peers has yet produced a gumboot chiton, a *Cryptochiton stelleri*. I really want one for my aquarium but that creature likes really cold water, like the ocean around Alaska, so I don't think anyone is going to get me one.

On the other side of the ledger, you'd see, if only you dared to come into my room despite "the stink," as put it, that my zoo is growing. I've taken possession of one water dragon, one sail-fin lizard, two caiman lizards, a few minnows, a handful of algae eaters, a gorgeous koi, and a baby allegator. Don't tell Mom that the alligator is actually an alligator. She thinks it's a lizard.

Also, like you, she thinks my room smells. So, she wants me to move my collection to one half of our garage. We're still negotiating. Our garage's combination of car exhaust, cold, and darkness would kill my babies.

Love,
Owen

****

Mar. 4, 1986
Rachel:

Well, that was abrupt! Frank's mom used to work in a pet store. When she came over to visit Mom, she said that she heard that I was fostering animals and asked to see them. Everything was great until she came upon my alligator and asked Mom if Mom knew what it was.

Mom shrugged and said, "a lizard."

Frank's mom corrected her.

Mom screamed. Dad, who had just gotten home from work, ran into my room and demanded, on the spot, that I release all my scaly friends at the closest pond. He even made me dump my tank of tropical fish, there, despite my protest that my fair weather beauties would get eaten or frozen within the day.

I demurred when Mom and Dad asked how I had amassed my collection and mumbled something about tutoring. Frank's mom admitted to having hired me but said nothing about how our agreement had quickly spoiled. I guess Mom and Dad figured I have lots of clients. I said nothing about trading baseball cards for critters.

Love,
Owen

****

Mar. 28, 1986
Sis:

From now on, you can call me "Owmapow." That's my superhero name. Do you like it?

Frank was picking on Janet during science class and I defended her. She told me I was a maladroit hero. I think she really *does* like me.

I picked out the name myself. Tomorrow, after lunch, I'll tell Janet my special name. Maybe, I'll make an eye mask and bring it to the cafeteria, too. Owmapow rides again!

Love,
Owmapow

****

Apr. 14, 1986
Rachel:

I can't believe you agreed to get your ears pierced. Ick! That's so unnatural.

I'm not complaining that you're a sister, not a brother. I certainly wouldn't want to live with someone like Frank's sibling and I certainly wouldn't want to be an only child like Janet.

But still, why put holes in your flesh? You're not even ten.

Please don't tell me that when you grow up, you're going to become artificially colored and flavored like Mom and her friends. Double ick!

In fairness, zebra fish and Aegean wall lizards, *Podarcis erhardii,* change color to attract mates, but you're much too young to get married. Who would you marry? Where would you live? How would you finish fourth grade?

Do you still talk to Betty, Cousin Liam's friend? She's also Jeremy Hudson's sister. Aren't you two in the same class? Doesn't Mom adore Betty's mom? Did Betty get her ears pierced, too? Triple ick.

Love,
~~Owen~~
Owmapow!

****

Apr. 27, 1986
Rachel:

As you know, my bringing my mask to school and showing it to
Janet did not turn out well. She didn't even sugarcoat her remarks
by lovingly calling me a "nitwit." She just made a face, spun, and
walked away with the group of girls that was waiting for her. All of
them, including Janet, pointed, and giggled.

All of them had pierce ears! Ick! I hope you don't grow up to be like
them. It's not nice to befriend a boy, and then, before he can even
ask you to the school dance, dump him.

Mr. Kashis, the science teacher, said I could have an afterschool
science club in the school lab. Unlike Mom and Dad, that grownup
understands the importance of making conjectures, deriving
logical consequence-type predictions from them, and then carrying
out experiments or empirical observations based on those prior
predictions. He also said that I could take over his job feeding the
principal's fish in the tank outside the principal's office and that I
could, under his jurisdiction, enter our city's science fair. Mr. Kashis
thinks I should research estuaries.

I wish you weren't grossed out by my ambassadors of nature. You're
a smart little sister and I could use someone to talk to.

Love,
~~Owen~~
Owmapow

****

May 4, 1986
Rachel:

I want to represent our city in the state science fair! That means that
I, Owmapow, have to win the city competition.

I will! The denizens of brackish water are swell, and some grownups think so, too.

The state fair's first prize, besides a thirty second slot on local cable TV, is a hundred dollars' worth of Chemcraft, Erector, and Glbert Lab supplies. I've heard rumors, too, that the winner gets to tour the biology and chemistry labs at our state university. Wow!

Owmapow

****

May 6, 1986
Rachel:

Frank's brother is taking Janet to the Ninth Grade Dance. So weird! She's my age, not a high schooler and her parents are letting her go.

When I stopped by the chess club, I heard Frank talking about their forthcoming date. He said something about Janet being more woman than most kids our age or his. I guess I never noticed. Now that I've noticed, I don't really care.

Meanwhile, during chess club, when Janet was about to checkmate a fellow, one of her blouse buttons flew open and everyone laughed. Janet buttoned up, turned red, and then left. The boys continued laughing.

Those fellows are so stupid! She's the second best player in our school. I wish I hadn't seen her get embarrassed. Serves me right for skipping fish patrol to play chess. After club hours, I had to ask the janitor to unlock the school's front door to let me out since I was so late feeding the principal's fish.

Owmapow

****

May 10, 1986
Rachel:

Did you ever have one of those days? Probably not. Mom and Dad love you.

Well, one of the principal's favorite fish died over the weekend. Mr. Kashis was mad and muttered something about my not even being on the job for a month.

What can I say? I was the one who spotted that little body floating at the top of the tank. If I had hid my observation, the other fish, too, could have died from the toxins that were leaking out of their tankmate.

Anyway, Mr. Kashis and I got into a row. He wants me to replace the fish with my own money. However, I think he saw the tear drip from my eye since he said he'd arrange a tutoring job, for pay, for me.

I thought about my limited experience with Frank's brother. I thought about Janet going to the dance with him. I thought about my invertebrates, amphibians, and reptiles getting dumped into the local waterway. I gave Mr. Kashis a polite "no."

I also withdrew my entry in the city science fair. I'd love to have my own set of lab equipment and I would love to teach myself engineering via an Erector Set. However, grownups, sometimes, are worse than peers. Instead of designing a science project, I'll stay in my room and read the books on marine life that I keep borrowing from our local library.

By the way, I'm also retiring my superhero mask. I'm not possessed of any special powers, except, perhaps, the ability to learn math quickly. Nah, that's not so special. Half of the chess team knows algebra. I think one or two of them knows geometry, too.

As per helping the world, I couldn't even save the scaly babies entrusted to my care. At least I no longer feel guilty about the baseball card trades I made.

Oh, and if you heard Dad yelling last night, that was because he discovered that I had taken a handful of cards from his boxes and had traded them for the very animals that he had made me toss. I guess he regretted making me a partner in crime in the deaths of innocent creatures.

Do you still want me to buy you silver-plated earrings for your birthday? It's important to accept people for who they are and not to try to make them not who we want them to be. I'm attempting to get my mind around the holes you made in your head.

Love,
Owmapow

Of Crustaceans and an Emerging Creative Writer

Dear Owen Brownstone:

All of us have read, reviewed, and discussed your story. We decided to pass on it. Although your story possesses a neat premise, it just didn't gain enough votes to secure a slot in our upcoming issue. We thank you for considering our publication and for allowing us the opportunity to review your work.

Also, per our submission guidelines, we are closed to speculative fiction. Our home page, Duotrop.com, and Ralan.com list this closure. We are, however, opened to flash. Thank you for your interest in our magazine.

An Associate Editor and Friends

****

Dear Associate Editor and Friends:

I am embarrassed. In my enthusiasm, I misread that datum. Please forgive me. Below, please find something else which is equally snarky, but half the length of my former submission, i.e., which is a bona fide flash. It qualifies for your magazine.

Owen Brownstone

****

Owen Brownstone:

We look forward to reading your story. Meanwhile, please supply us with the missing information.

An Associate Editor and Friends

****

Dear Associate Editor and Friends:

I don't understand what constitutes "missing information." The body of "The Care and Feeding of Rabid Hedgehogs" is 627 words. My complete contact information is below. My preferred by-line is "Owen Brownstone." The story is, again, pasted below.

I hope I am getting the submission process right. I'm sorry for all the time that my entry is costing you. I hope that my story proves to be a small compensation for your extended efforts.

Owmapow
(Owen Brownstone)

PS: Below, please find links to some of my other, recent electronic publications.

****

Owmapow:

That's better. Always check format and be sure to include contact information on all your submissions to EVERY market—especially those that pay for stories.

Your submission has been forwarded to the rest of the staff. When we have all read, reviewed, and discussed your story, we will email you our decision. Our response time is about two months. We are currently reading for the October/November issue and for future issues. Thank you for your interest in our magazine!

Filigree Lucca
Associate Editor

****

Filigree Lucca:

You've been a sweetheart throughout this process. Thanks!

Yours will be my first paid short story publication. I've been paid in other genres. I've been published, in this genre in exchange for copies, but I have never been paid cash in this genre. I'm very excited about the acceptance! Thanks!!!

Owmapow

****

Owmapow:

Congrats on your first sale! If you have another story coming out before we publish "The Care and Feeding of Rabid Hedgehogs," please let us know. We do honor first sales but can't give you that specific honor if "The Care and Feeding of Rabid Hedgehogs," is not your first sale.

Forward your PayPal info to us as soon as you can, so we can update our records.

Filigree and Friends

****

Filigree and Friends:

In a word, "coooool!" It is my pleasure to be able to help creep out your readers. My bio. is below. My PayPal data are below, too. Please let me know when I can send you other work. I'm grateful to have "The Care and Feeding of Rabid Hedgehogs" accepted by your publication!

Owmapow

PS: You are one of the best/encouraging/helpful editors I have ever worked with. Do you want intermittent updates on my publications? (I publish under several versions of my name, from "Owen Brownstone" to "Owmapow B." to "Dr. Owen B." to "Dr. Owen Brownstone," etc.)

Which publication rights is *Smarmy Friends* claiming? No matter. After the holidays, I plan to work on my website. Would you post a link to my website next to my story?

Meanwhile, I am cold calling publishers by mailing them full book manuscripts. Watch out world! Owmapow rides again!

****

Owmapow:

Oh my!! I am just now seeing this email! No clue as to why it didn't pop up before. Anyway, regular updates would be great! Also feel free to add a bio. to each submission. As far as publication rights, if you mouse over our submissions page, you will see our terms of service (our nitty gritty). Writers at *Smarmy Friends* retain their copyrights. We just get non-exclusive first print rights.

You can promote your website when it's up. Having links from an external site is a nice way to get crawled by Google sooner and to get a decent PageRank earlier, so I highly recommend sending links. Thank you for the generous comments! I have worked with a wild mix of editors myself (some very good, most very bad).

Filigree and Friends

****

Filigree and Friends:

I meant what I said about you as an editor. I have worked with
wonderful people, and I have worked with idiots.

Per the rights, that's good. I'm thinking of compiling my work into
a book. I would like to use the story I wrote for you as part of that
collection. Of course, credit will be given to *Smarmy Friends* in the end
matter.

Crazed Critters, Thank G-d, just accepted a poem of mine for future
publication. I'm linking you to the bio. that I wrote for them since
it's more up to date that the one that I sent to you. I never know
what to say about myself. If any of these data are useful, feel free to
use them.

I must get my website up. I also need to find an agent. I'm
proceeding a bit backwards.

Speaking of which, I choose to take all your remarks about
banners, linking URLS, and the like as encouragement to learn to
"fix the windshield wipers." Thanks! Please keep your comments
flowing!

Happy Holidays!
Owmapow

****

Jackie Mashbly:

I just had "The Care and Feeding of Rabid Hedgehogs" published
in *Smarmy Friends* and "The Elephant's Toe" published in *Crazed
Critters*. Now, I'd like to publish "Squamata's Big Dance" in your
venue, *Squeaks and Roars*. To wit, below, please find my short
story, "Squamata's Big Dance." Please let me know if it suits you.

Let me know, as well, when you need a bio., web links, or other information. Thanks for considering my writing.

Owmapow Brownstone

****

Owmapow:

Thanks for your submission! We at *Squeaks and Roars* will post your work in our February, online issue. Welcome to our menagerie!

Jackie

****

Jackie:

I enjoyed reading all of February's pieces. I would like to reply to the people who posted about my entry. Am I permitted to provide links to other works?

Owmapow

****

Owmapow:

Sorry I'm late getting back to you. These have been a busy couple of days. Regarding the submission rules, I need to have them, but I'm also as flexible as possible, since I want *Squeaks and Roars* to be a great, supportive experience for its writers. It's hard enough to take all the thwacks that writers must take. I'm not interested in adding to them.

I hear your frustrations with writing. When I was a teenager and when I was in college, I used to submit to literary magazines. These days, those outlets seems to be dwindling. I'm not sure that short stories are of much use, anymore. They're good for getting some publishing credits, but the opportunities seem to be drifting to web publication, and I'm not sure that agents give as much credence to them as to full-length books. However, *Squeaks and Roars* has been listed in (successful) query letters. How cool is that?!

For a writing career today (that pays), I think the only real route to break in is via a novel. After a successful novel, you could probably do a short story compilation, but all your serious efforts should probably be directed at novel writing. I'd also focus on only one project at a time. Agents don't like to hear that you've got a bunch on your desk. It makes them wonder why your bunches haven't sold.

If you have tried to query those manuscripts and they haven't placed, I'd set them aside for now and start a new project. Try super hard to correct whatever things you think caused your past books not to sell. Unfortunately, we have to be reader-oriented.

Thanks for the emails!

Jackie

PS: Would you like a biographical note to appear at the end of your piece or would you like a link to be placed at your by-line? Just tell me what you want.

****

Jackie:

Thanks for your candor. Sometimes, I get frustrated with the publication process.

It seems like I have a lot to think about. I certainly don't want to make bad choices.

I enjoyed your web comments. Do you do pen and ink art? I make ceramics, use found art in sculptures and paint.

A friend suggested that I offer writing workshops. I've advertised, accordingly, and received a nominal response. I might run them anyway, just to garner a local reputation.

I need to find ways to stand out from the crowd. I want to get into status publications and to make some money from writing. I know, I know, so does everyone's kid sister, misplaced aunt, and formerly dead cousin. Any ideas that you have are welcomed.

I'm not sure what's next. I love writing, in general, and creating havoc with words, more specifically. I've begun a series of short stories about a chimera and its keeper, have several books that are waiting for the right prince, I mean agent, have a chapbook in the wings, and am creating a collection of tales about an incorrigible teenager.

Any guidance, encouragement, etc. that you could spare would be welcomed. I look forward to your next email

Keep in touch!
Owmapow

****

Dear Editor:

It's not just plants that have rhythms. In the following essay, "Weeding," the beauty of the natural sequence of discovery, both among green friends, and within oneself, is explicated. Too often we are so focused on results, whether those ends are a cure for an ailment or irritant, or a means of catapulting us to a new level of understanding, that we forget that, in the progression of the natural world, it is at least as important to get lost among the brambles as it is to achieve socially recognized goals.

I hope you enjoy "Weeding." I think you will like the wordplay at the end. I look forward to hearing from you.

Sincerely,
Owen Brownstone

Owen Brownstone has had "The Care and Feeding of Rabid Hedgehogs" published in *Smarmy Friends*, "The Elephant's Toe" published in *Crazed Critters*, and "Squamata's Big Dance" posted in *Squeaks and Roars*. He hopes to place his book about a chimera and its keeper with a New York City press.

****

Dear Owen:

"Weeding" is a very nice piece. Unfortunately, it does not fit our editorial needs for the coming year. We do not currently have a place to publish essays, other than "Earthly Beasts," which is written by a single contributor. I want to add a department to include works such as yours, but right now, we don't have the pages to do so.

I am sure you will find a publisher because your piece is lovely. Thank you for your interest in our publication.

Best Wishes,
Valarie Rose

****

Dear Dr. Owen Brownstone:

Your application to be a Contributing Writer to our website has been declined for one of the following reasons: your writing suggested a first-person, experiential, or opinion-based approach to material rather than an objective journalistic style that quotes verifiable sources, your writing sample contained errors in language use, structure, grammar, spelling, or voice, or your writing did not reflect the search interests of our Internet audience. Also possible was that your educational and employment experience did not suggest authoritative expertise in the subject areas you wish to cover.

Due to volume of applicants and limited editorial staff and time, we are unable to field inquiries requesting more specific reasons for declining this application. We reserve the right to select our contract writers according to our mandate. We wish you the best with your writing career on a site more suited to your interests and abilities.

Creatures and Flowers

****

Dear *Creatures and Flowers* Editor:

Bunk! I have a Ph.D. in biology with a specialty in the order *Decapoda*. I have taught thousands of university students how to write research papers. What's more, I've been interviewed by the mass media and have quite a few academic publications. I invite you to explain to me how my samples or my background are insufficient for your needs.

The sample I sent to you, "Weeding," was vetted by another publication that merely couldn't fit it into its forthcoming issue. What's more, if you bothered to verify my credentials, you would have noted that I had "The Care and Feeding of Rabid Hedgehogs" published in *Smarmy Friends,* "The Elephant's Toe" published in *Crazed Critters,* and "Squamata's Big Dance" in *Squeaks and Roars.*

Dr. Owen Brownstone

****

Dear John Danderwoof:

"Thank-you for accepting "Weeding." I now understand why, despite your letter of acceptance, the piece never made it to print.

Specifically, in cleaning up my email files, I came to realize that I had corresponded with you through several of my appellations; "Dr. Owen Brownstone," the name I use professionally, "Owmapow Brownstone," the name I formerly used professionally, and "Owmapow," my everyday name. Short of onomatology, there is little reason to correspond thusly—I slipped. I hope I did not cause you too much confusion.

To that end, I am writing to clarify that all the above nomenclature is mine and that it was me who is indeed the author of "Weeding" as well as of a second piece, "Crustaceans in Deep Space." Did you receive the second piece? Did you like it? Do you want to publish it, as well? When might "Weeding" see print?

Owmapow (Owen Brownstone)

****

Owmapow:

Well, your "Crustaceans in Deep Space" was most interesting. It will appear in *Astral Flora and Fauna* 21. Have a look at the document attached, and if you have any questions, please get back to me. "Weeding," now that I you have clarified that you are its author, will appear in *Astral Flora and Fauna* 20. I hope to see more of your writing.

John Danderwoof

****

Dear John Danderwoof:

I am sorry that it has taken me so long to get back to you. The three references that contained "n.d.s," have been resolved to the best of my ability. The first one, the 2011 cite, needed a shallow dig into an HTML. The second one, the c. 2013 reference, was an archaeological tour of webpages that no longer exist. The third reference, too, no longer exists in its 2014 form, so I changed it to reflect that datum's new webpage (which, incidentally, boasts similar content). Sigh.

The above aside, I am grateful you accepted that second piece of my writing. Thank-you for your compliments. I look forward to hearing from you.

Sincerely,
Owmapow

****

Hi John:

Thanks for the update. I guess I am still just a little confused. The table of contents says 2014 but the cover says 2015. Which one is it?

Owmapow

****

Owmapow:

Oh, my! Yes, that is a little confusing. But take heart, the error you identify applies only to a wrong attachment, not to the actual forthcoming, 2015 issue. Truly thanks for alerting me to the blunder. How do you like the outside front cover?

Again, I'm glad to have two of your works for *Astral Flora and Fauna's* 2015 issues. Please send more.

John

****

John:

Although I have enjoyed a glorious career as a writer with "Weeding" and "Crustaceans in Deep Space" appearing in your fine publication and with, respectively, "The Care and Feeding of Rabid Hedgehogs" in *Smarmy Friends*, "The Elephant's Toe" in *Crazed Critters*, and "Squamata's Big Dance" in *Squeaks and Roars*, I have decided to give up on creative text and to invest more of my non-academic time in fashioning sculptures made from found art.

Thank-you for your ongoing support. I will always cherish your friendship.

Owmapow

Deep Sea Mothers

Hi Owmapow:

I'm sitting here eating calamari. Our site just went live on Monday, and I've been extremely busy with it and haven't really had time to respond to email until tonight.

I'm wondering if it would be possible for you to write a "guest" post to be released Sunday? I'd have you write it by Thursday and then I'd post it ahead so that it would appear on Sunday. I'm thinking of adding you to the line-up of writers who post every other weekend. Would you be OK with that?

We have ten writers at present, which has filled our current roster, but I enjoyed your writing so much I'd like to know if you would be interested in being an alternate for those times when people are on vacation or are unable to post for one reason or another.

Right now, we're posting every other week, five days a week. It's important for some of the other writers to have their posts up for twenty-four hours, so this is what I've agreed to, for now. Once the site is settled, we're planning to revisit posting on weekends. In the meantime, tell me what you think.

Manny Olsen
Editor, *Waving at Biology*

****

Dear Manny:

I read the "About Us" section of your site. The *Waving at Biology* writers are poignant and funny! I'd love to be on your bench; I'd be honored to "warm seats" for such a team. Thanks for the opportunity. While I "bat temp.," I could also defrost fish, wash peppers, and empty sinkfuls of dishes.

Is there any compensation beyond a by-line? Also, if possible, please tell me how much lead time I'll have and the length of entries you seek, when I'm needed as a substitute. I look forward to participating.

Owmapow

PS: How did you find your agent? I noticed you had a book published with one of the Big Five New York houses.

****

Owmapow:

You pick the topic. The length can be anything from one hundred to five hundred words, depending on what you're writing about. Just make it funny. We've had a series of heavy posts recently. Email your work to me. I'll edit and post it.

My agent sought me.

Manny

****

Dear Owmapow:

I am so confused. The blog, to which you were assigned, is called

"Modern Squid." The post you wrote was titled "Another Time, Another Teuthida." But I don't understand why you want all your work to be listed under "Far Shores." I can't change the blog's name. It's an established blog. I think we're having a semantic difference.

The blog is the name of the entire entity. Each "article" is a post. Each post is subsumed by the blog, itself. If you look at the blog, it should make sense to you. There isn't any place to add another title.

Anyway, I've got your post queued for Sunday morning. I'd like you to fill in on alternate weeks. The sort of writing we're looking for has the same tone as do those pieces you sent links for at *Smarmy Friends* and at *Crazed Critters*.

Manny

****

Manny:

I agree, it's semantics. I also agree that it's important to validate the variety of life that exists in the sea. So, I'd like to call all my contributions "Far Shores," even if they are incorporated under "Modern Squid."

Am I correct in understanding that you want me to send you another piece in about two weeks?

Owmapow

****

Hi Manny!

Below, please find "No More Green Pollutants" for today, June 12th, and "Nurturing Your Pet Cephalopod," for my next installment, on June 26th.

I'm off to the American Institute of Biological Sciences annual meeting. I'll send more blog entries to you when I return.

Warm Wishes,
Owmapow

PS: Is it possible to put more space (another blank line) between leads/intros. and actual entries? Current formatting bleeds the two together and makes reading a little confusing.

PPS: On what basis did your agent seek you?

****

Owmapow:

Hello. Yes, that's no problem. I will approve the one for now and the other for next Thursday.

As far as the intros. bleeding into the body, I don't see that on any of my browsers. Which browser do you use? Are you able, by chance, to capture a screen shot? I don't want that sort of problem!

Thanks!
Manny

****

Manny:

I've returned! Sadly, my pet cuttlefish died while I was away. Pardon me while I contemplate just how many lobster molts my nautili need for dinner, how I will help my "adopted" *Cirrina* find a mate, and why humanity has allowed noise pollution to impair the repopulating of giant squids.

Owmapow

****

Owmapow:

Your last article was about raising turtles. Your submissions must be about molluscans. While I liked that piece, it does not suit the blog's content. Please write and submit something else.

Manny

****

Manny:

Your July 12th posting was poignant and well written. You are a person from whom many cephalopod enthusiasts can learn. You are a succinct writer, too.

However, I need to end our relationship. First, it remains important to me to validate the variety of life that exists in the sea. Second, the pieces I submitted to you were neither published nor acknowledged, except for the first one. Third, almost half of a dozen of my emails to you have gone unanswered.

If I do not hear from you by tomorrow, please understand that I withdraw my offer of "Internalized Molluscan Shells," "The Seven Wonders of World Nautili" and "Testudines for Children."

Sincerely,
Owmapow

****

Owmapow!

"Bent Antennules" and "Magnificent Crawfish" are in the new issue of *Ocean Scavengers*!

Could I prevail on you for a small favor? You recently did that eBook thing. We're preparing an eBook imprint but have no packaging with which to work. Might you send me a tactfully bowdlerized copy of your paperwork? I'll keep the particulars secret.

Barnaby Gray

****

Barnaby:

Thank-you for accepting my poetry. Yikes, my eBook contract for *Crustaceans Never End* was rolled into a contract with audio and print components from my publisher. Would you like me to "introduce" you to her? My experience is that most small presses help each other.

Also, why are you keeping secrets? That aside, would you like to consider some of my gathered work for an eBook? I am envisioning a poetry collection entitled *Hedgehogs and Lobsters*.

Owmapow

****

Owmapow:

We crustacean lovers are born conspirators. As one of our treasured poets, we'd welcome work from you at Ocean Scavengers Inc. (we've already got a collection from Syria and a dual language thing from a young Croatian!)

That rolled together contract sounds perfect. We're not anticipating audio and print, but we ought not to dismiss that potential. I'm uncomfortable about asking competitors for help. Whatever you've got would work just fine, if you're comfortable sharing.

Barnaby

****

Oh Barnaby!

Please take this email in the caring way it is intended.

First, you are magnificent in acquiring funding, attracting writers, and aiding writers on their journeys. May you succeed for decades! I, for one, adore *Ocean Scavengers* and the empowerment it represents.

Second, get yourself a lawyer. There are nasty people in the publishing world. The nasties tend to stay low until they sniff out the possibility of making money off some innocent (all of us, to one degree or another, are innocent.) Once you announce to the world that you are producing eBooks, you will be considered fair game to such horrible individuals.

Contracts are meant to protect both the publisher and the writer, even and especially with convergent media products. An eBook contract will have clauses about prior publication of content, length of contract, fair use of materials, etc. etc. There is far too much that must be covered for me to give all the details in a letter. Also, specifics necessarily vary from publisher to publisher. A document that seems fair to both parties often is fair.

A few hours of a lawyer's time, now, will save you much heartache and expense later. Ask him or her to help you fashion a "boilerplate" contract. Make sure that you hire someone experienced with eBook publishing contracts. The domain of print has different rights and different laws than does the electronic one.

Third, join your peers. There are many, many indie publisher orgs., including, but not limited to; Small Publishers Association of North America, American Amateur Press Association, Small Press Exchange, Consortium Book Sales and Distribution, and Council of Literary Magazines and Presses.

Members of these and of similar groups can help you, usually *gratis*, steer yourself to profit and to a continued good reputation. They can advise you of the legal and financial pitfalls they have encountered or avoided. It's worthwhile connecting with folks who have already succeeded in accomplishing your goals.

Fourth, the writers you have in the pipe, for eBooks, sound wonderful. However, hold on long enough, before offering them Atlantis, to cover yourself, i.e., to secure your own underwater kingdom! You have worked hard to attract subordinate editors who know a thing or two about manuscripts and have worked hard to build your stable of writers. As you know, branding is everything. Keep your name above the surface and you will likely grow and grow.

I would love to send a proposal to you, but I will wait until you have figured out a few essentials. I want, very much, for your new venture to be wonderful for you!

Invest a little now and reap much later.

Please forgive my concern for your well-being. I DO care that you succeed wildly. Let me know what happens.

Warmly,
Owmapow

****

Peter:

Who are you? Are you the healer from Boston with the Yale education? The regular contributor to *The Ocean View*? The writer with multiple book publications, including a mention in *The New York Times*? Someone else? Googling you yielded several people with the same first and last name as yours.

Depending on who you are, there might be opportunities to study with me beyond my "invitation only" class. Furthermore, it's a good idea, and one with which you are familiar, whether you are the doctor, the reporter, or the novelist, to investigate, where possible, anyone with whom you are building bridges.

I Look Forward to Hearing More from You,
Owen Brownstone, Ph.D.
(Owmapow)

****

Peter:

Thanks for resending. You are welcome in my regular writing courses during the period in which you will be in California. Ping me a bit closer to your flight and I will send you links to readings and homework assignments. Writing about the seas is a very serious business.

You're a tough cookie, so I'm supposing that you won't be daunted by the insights of students who have been with me for multiple courses or by the lack of bluffing or trivia spouted by those writers. Meanwhile, I hope the intervening span is a pleasant one for you. I look forward to hearing from you in a few months.

Owmapow

****

Owmapow:

The last email went through before I finished it.

Thanks for this email. I did find your last email provocative and somewhat hostile, not because I'm "vulnerable," but because my philosophy towards writing is different from yours. For starters, I take great pride in being a doctor (not a "doctor").

I wish the answer to your question about what I hope to gain from writing could be neatly divided into "insight" OR "renown" OR "riches." I have different goals with different projects. Gaining and sharing insights is always a goal. Renown is always welcome; I'm not a writer who pretends not to care if anyone reads my work. What's more, money is always welcomed. I have a back-burner project, a bent genre story that could be profitable when I finish it.

Making my boundaries clear, I don't feel a particular need, at this point, to explain to you my reasons for wanting to publish, what it is about my work that makes me proud, or why I sometimes spend summers in Santa Barbara. I would, however, be happy to share my thoughts with you when I get to know you better.

I'm confident about my writing. I value people who will tell me when they perceive my ideas are trite or will lead nowhere. Your insights about the pitfalls of basing a narrative on an actual case are most welcome.

I'd like to take your workshops. I'm still figuring out my dates for my trip. I believe I'll be in Los Angeles for part of the summer. So, I would like to be part of the second half of Descriptive Writing and the first half of Dialogue Writing (a skill I must hone). The price is not a problem.

Peter

****

Peter:

I'm pretty sure I expressed my boundaries much more strongly than they needed to be stated. I apologize.

Lately, I've had many folks contacting me. They want something for nothing or want me to transform their raw goods "magically" into finished products. I am sincerely sorry if you became the recipient of my screed simply because you were next in line. I still value good character traits above all else and still hold myself accountable when my actions are less than admirable.

Whereas I can't include you in the advanced class (the students that I selected for that class are at a different proficiency level than you), I could make two offers to you.

1. I can allow you prorated entrance to my weekly workshops (usually, I only allow people to enter for a full course so as not to disrupt other participants.) I've made this exception before, but generally do so very rarely. Each class meeting costs twenty-five dollars.

2. I could work with you privately on a set of skills or on a project. Given my full schedule, I'm less inclined to tender this option. I usually charge very modestly and hardly ever take on private students. Believe it or not, my regular work is in marine biology.

Again, I am sincerely sorry for how I responded to you. I should have realized, immediately, especially for an accomplished individual like yourself that seeking instruction is an act of vulnerability.

Humbly,
Owmapow

PS: Look at my "Another Time, Another Teuthida" and "Nurturing Your Pet Cephalopod," in *Waving at Biology*, and at my "Bent Antennules" in *Ocean Scavengers*. Worldly goings-on and artistic expression can and must coexist.

Owmapow Gets Fired

Owmapow:

I started writing in the 1970s, when I couldn't find a job. I never planned to be a writer. The first thing I submitted was accepted by *Snails and Puppy Dog Tails*. My other publications followed.

Rena

****

Rena:

Wow! You have been publishing for a long time. As for me, I've been a biology professor for a long time.

As per writing, I'm a bit spoiled by the ease of doing business electronically. I just wish I had more acceptances.

In other matters, are you or any of the folks in your circles interested in a creative writing workshop? My newest ad is attached. Please pass it around to your friends and colleagues.

Let's keep the conversation going. I'd love to hear about your writing success.

Owmapow

****

Owmapow:

All of us are spoiled by electronics. The computer revolution has changed publishing. I live in a sparsely populate region of Montana but am read in Bangkok and Sydney.

Also, I'm a seasoned writer. Not only do I write short fiction, but I likewise worked in journalism for two plus decades. I've written everything from light features to political analysis to social satire. My book manuscripts are making the rounds, too. I'm offering a novel and a poetry chapbook.

Cheers,
Rena

****

Rena:

May you always know success! I just filed my taxes. Also, I just had at batch of receipts printed for when I teach writing. Maybe, one day, I'll teach online. For today, face-to-face suits me.

In the past, I taught narrative at a continuing education program, and I taught business writing at the local YMCA. I've been blogging for *Shellfish and Their Landlocked Buddies* and for the children's science site, *Under the Sea.* I've additionally been published in *Smarmy Friends, Squeaks and Roars, Crazed Critters,* and in other modest venues. This summer, alone, I've had almost half of a dozen poems, short stories and essays accepted for publication.

Additionally, I've been selected to judge a creative nonfiction contest for *Ocean Scavengers*, am in talks to ghost for someone with an Internet presence and am happily moving toward formalizing my business of writing workshops. Are you or any of the folks in your circles interested in a creative writing seminar?

Owmapow

****

Owmapow:

My income is mostly from translating and editing, although I recently began writing, again, for *Tails of Pet Wonder*. I don't write for them too often since they pay so poorly.

The demise of print media is a world-wide phenomenon. Today, it's hard to make a living from print. The electronic media are worse. There is more money in business writing than in creative writing. If you are already teaching science writing and are already established as an academic, why are you trying to get more involved in creative work?
Rena

****

Rena:

I have several book projects on hold (I've turned down at least one publisher because his contract's terms were crummy) and am trying to find time to send in more manuscripts to more editors I'm starting to get a rhythm, but truth be told, I'd rather create and refine than promote. Also, I've taught two science writing workshops.

Creative work is freeing. Academic work is not.
Owmapow

PS: Googling me will only give you a portion of my work since I publish under several variations of my name ;) My motivation for using multiple monikers sits somewhere between my need to protect my identity and my having "established" an academic presence before becoming a creative writer. So, I'm "out there" in several versions, not all of which I have revealed even to my sister who, recently, crowed that she had located a piece of my online poetry.

Since I believe convergent media are powerful, I don't really want to give anyone all my pieces.

****

Owmapow:

Wow. I'm impressed. NSF scholar, huh? A *few* novels in progress?! Crustaceans? That's a heavy topic. What are chemical setae? How do they function on a lobster? I know science writing is more lucrative than creative work, but I find it to be boring and repetitive. I flunked high school chemistry. You're probably good at Science Writing, though.

Rena

****

Rena:

Don't be impressed. I'm currently running in loops, not being sure of which way to apply myself and am feeling very, very frustrated. Writing novels isn't publishing them. Also, I grew up calling creative nonfiction "expository writing."

I like science writing. I did a piece, last year, for John Hopkins' *Arts and Sciences Magazine*. It's fun to explain complex ideas to the lay public.

As per "science writing," I dislike it per se. I'm not very interested in machines. Most "science" writing, presently, is user manual work for computers.

In terms of writing fiction, I need to hook myself to a star. After two days of acceptance letters, I am getting rejection letters, again. Sigh. Maybe I'll try working as a writing professor. Are you or any of the folks in your circles interested in a creative writing workshop?

My newest ad is attached. Please pass it around to your friends and colleagues.

Owmapow

****

To Whom It May Concern:

Beam me up and then slather my mind with the marshmallows that melt while being used to build pretzel stick carbon rings. It's a pity that my platypi were mistaken for chimeras, but most creatures that are possessed of characteristics of several classes get confused with each other. Alternatively, we can join together to employ telescopes using coded aperture masks and seek out life on Mars.

In all or partial seriousness, hire me, a biology professor to write pop science articles. Links to some of my published work and my CV are available on request. Together, we can explore the physics of why G sharp and A flat are dissimilar and the chemistry of making a chocolate cake. Fly me.

Owen Brownstone

****

Hi Owen,

Nice note. The site's called CreatureComforts.com. Feel free to check it out. I would love to receive a few writing samples. I also need to confirm that you live in Canada for you to be eligible for this job.

Zayne

****

Zayne:

Bummer. Not a Canadian. How 'bout someone who is a citizen of the good ole US of A? Meanwhile, are you or any of the folks in your circles interested in a creative writing workshop? My newest ad is attached. Please pass it around to your friends and colleagues.

Owen

****

Owen:

Sorry, Owen. I can't hire Americans. Good luck!

Zayne

****

Zayne:

If you hear of anything that's suitable for me, please send it my way. The offer for the creative writing workshop is still good, though.

Owen Brownstone

****

Hi Owen:

Your online course, Viruses and Larger Animals, sounded amazing. However, I think I have made a mistake. I am very sorry, but I think I have overextended myself. We have just moved, and I am juggling graduate school as well as looking after a pregnant hedgehog. I am starting my own business, too. As much as I would love to complete your course right now, I do not think I would be able to dedicate the time and headspace it deserves.

I realize you said there are no refunds. However, I was wondering if you could make an exception just this once? I appreciate your time and I apologize for any inconvenience.

Sincerely,
Cindy Smithers

****

Cindy:

I hope your move went well. I'm sorry. I can't issue a refund. Graduate school is tough. Pregnant hedgehogs are demanding. I can commiserate with the former and can offer links, depending on the issue, to people and places (I've found a strong support team to be essential when nurturing animals) for the latter.

As per the class, you can choose not to participate at all, or you can choose to participate in a way that matches your resources (e.g., you can do readings, participate in discussions, answer only the prompts for which you have time.) You're a grown woman, so you've probably heard what I am next going to say, but I'll say it, anyway. If you don't nurture yourself, you can't nurture those around you.

On balance, brisk walks, container gardening or some other item might be what fosters you best. Maybe biology courses are fun for you. I don't know you, so I can't guess.

The first year in graduate school is one that is normally tear-filled. My mentor was mentored, in turn, by someone else. It's a tough transition. Good for you for persevering!

I'm working on a book's galley proofs today and will be checking my email intermittently. If you want to write back about your pregnant hedgehogs, I'm here for you.

Warmly,
Owen

****

Owen:

Thank you for your support and for all your wonderful graduate school advice. It is a tough gig, but as you said, the first year is toughest, so I am hanging in there. I would love to be in contact with experts on pregnant hedgehogs.

I hear that you cannot issue a refund. I understand. However, right now it would be very stressful for me to participate even at half mast, so to speak.

As a compromise, would I be able to participate in the next course you offer instead, i.e., could you hold my payment in escrow until then? I would really appreciate that. Thank-you, again, for all your advice!

Cindy

****

Cindy:

I am sincerely sorry, but I do not set aside credit for students. I offer classes as my publishing schedule permits (sometimes regularly, sometimes, not) and try to do as little bookkeeping and other record maintenance as possible. That is to say, although I lose 10% of funds by using PayPal, I employ that system so that legal records are created for me and so that I don't have to use up my temporal resources on accounting.

Speaking of which, I must return to the manuscript at hand. You are welcome to participate or not and to do so as much as you desire.

Owen

****

Hi Owen!

Oh, that is a shame. I hoped to attend whenever I could, but it will not really be my maximum attention, at this time.

Cindy

****

Dear Faculty:

On a somber note, the employment of Drs. Tim Atkins, Own Brownstone, Dana Fellman, Sam Handler, Sara Polsky, Jennifer Suku, and Paula Thesu at our institution ended, today.

As you know, all their contracts were not renewed. Those teachers had entered a labor dispute with our university. As part of the labor dispute, they did not hand in their class grades. As a result, the administration cannot allow them to teach even summer courses.

The greatest asset any educational institution has is its faculty. Today, our university has lost some GREAT assets. Their commitment, dedication and experience will be sorely missed.

Dean Gerald Hargity

****

Dear Friends:

You've got to give Tim, Owen, Dana, and the rest of the crew credit for dedication, commitment, AND experience and for great professionalism under fire. I am saddened that it has ended in this way... No, I'm sickened. What happens now to students' grades will be left up to the department's executive committee.

Sally Norman,
Department Chair

****

Dear Dr. Sally Norman:
CC: Dean Gerald Hargity

At present, my life, unfortunately, remains lackluster. Over and over, I find myself sucking in my breath when visiting the campus. Is there really no way to reinstate me to my position?

A younger professor might not care about the administration's response to our action, but I had less than a decade until retirement. What's more, I never did earn enough to justify being treated so harshly.

All that I had grasped was that in the good ol' US of A, work stoppages are not legally punishable and that good lawyers, alongside of union leaders, can protect their clients from illicit firings. Further, it seems wrong that no matter how well placed my scholarship has been in academic journals, and that no matter, for many years, my students evaluated me as teaching at the highest level of excellence, the university has no more need for me.

I even dutifully fulfilled the public service requirement of my job. For five years, I educated the public about deep sea creatures at *Shellfish and Their Landlocked Buddies* and at the children's science site, *Under the Sea*. Surely, the administration meant to reprimand rather than to dismiss me.

Dr. Owen Brownstone

****

Mr. Kevin Smith:

Good morning! Attached is my CV. I qualify for the Professor of Humanities position you ae representing. Even though my Ph.D. is in Marine Biology and Ecology, during the last decade, I have taught science writing courses. I presented research on science writing at national conferences, too. The last academic book that I was working on was on a topic intersecting both science and communication.

Which school is offering the job? Is the position full-time or part-time? Please send more information.

Thanks!
Owen Brownstone, Ph.D.

****

Kevin:

Is the school in Pasadena? Santa Barbara? In an area between the two cities? It's not wise for me, at this point in my creative life, to commute too far from home, or to take on too many hours of work. For me, "part-time" and "relatively local" are highly desirable attributes in a teaching position.

[The following paragraph is confidential; please do not forward these data to the employer who is offering the Professor of Humanities position]

Elsewhere, I signed a paper (I'm not sure if it is binding, since it was not a contract, stating that I would give priority to working, part-time, at a local institute of higher education, in science writing, beginning Fall 2017. The assumptions undergirding this very informal agreement are that the program would be approved by the school's board of trustees, and that I would master sufficient competence in rhetoric to lecture on the necessary topics.

Regardless, I would like to return to the classroom and to my program of research. I am a trained academic with a modest publication record. As well, I need income. My cash reserves will soon be depleted. Meanwhile, I am continuing to blog on biology for a children's science website, to submit writing projects to additional scholarly outlets and to strengthen my knowledge of rhetorical theory and criticism (my sister, who is also an academic, is helping me with this last item.)

I look forward to your email about the matter of the other school. Perhaps you can answer my questions, if only obliquely.

Sincerely,
Owen Brownstone, Ph.D.

****

Dr. Owen Brownstone:

I was asked not to give out the name of the institution, yet. They're in the preliminary stages of looking for candidates, so it may take some time until you hear from them. The position may start out part-time and increase—it's not been determined yet.

Best Regards,
Kevin Smith
Associate Director of Employment

****

Owen:

It's in Pasadena, but this would be for down the road—possibly next fall. So, I searched, and the dean is a woman. I do not know her. I suggest you contact her directly. The description of the job is what I already sent you.

Kevin Smith
Associate Director of Employment

****

Kevin:

Thanks! I have an informal interview set for Tuesday.

Owen

****

Owen:

Great! Please keep me updated!

Best regards,
Kevin Smith
Associate Director of Employment

****

Dear Dr. Anita Lata:

I am writing in response to your posting for a professor. I have long been part of the academic avant-garde. My professional life includes both award-winning work in marine biology, and, as of late, in science writing. My educational method is interdisciplinary; my thinking, writing, and teaching are introspective. Whereas my research foci have evolved over the decades, my emphasis remains on individual and collective communication accountability.

Attached are my cover letter, my CV, my references, and samples of my publications. When you are ready for additional information, please contact me.

Sincerely,
Owen Brownstone, Ph.D.

****

Kevin,

[for your eyes only]
The meeting was a disappointment. It turned out to be an information interview, which I expected. However, it seemed that the other party wanted information from me, not vice versa, and when my "professional" opinion did not meet her expectations, i.e., when she couldn't use any more of my time without paying me for it, she ended our meeting.

Owen

****

Owen,

I'm sorry to hear that it was disappointing. Thanks for letting me know. We'll keep trying!

Best regards,
Kevin Smith
Associate Director of Employment

****

Rena:

Below is a copy of the letter I sent to that dean. I think the message expresses the first point. The second point, though more subtle, is present, too.

In sum:
1. I am annoyed that I was taken advantage of.
2. That dean has no idea how valuable I am/could be to her.

Your Tail-Swishing (think of cats) Friend,

Owmapow

Dr. Anita Lata:

Thank-you for taking the time to meet with me, yesterday. Attached please find a self-explanatory curriculum design for your proposed program.

In a former life, I minored in higher education, served on curriculum development committees, chaired the instructional development research group of a regional biological sciences organization, and wrote/presented/published papers on related topics.

The attached is a quick "doddle" of ideas. If you are interested, I could point you to lots of sources, organizations, and more. However, only this attachment is a free sample. Thereafter, like everyone else, I charge.

Owen Brownstone, Ph.D.

****

Kevin:

So, meanwhile, what is the next step that I should take with that college, which proceeded without me? Can you contact the school's president, on my behalf? In the spring of 2016, I signed that paper that committed me to serving on its teaching staff for three years, beginning in the fall of 2017. The president's office will have my signed document.

Owen

****

Owen:

This is outrageous! I cannot believe how badly you have been treated (by so many employers). I'm guessing that this is an issue in the humanities (getting as much as possible for as little as possible), but it still rots.

Rena

Rena:

This is another of the "hits" I took. The email, below is the curt response I got when I asked why the program, to which I had attached my name and credibility, allegedly, for three years, began without me!

****

Dear Dr. Owen Brownstone:

I am not that involved anymore. Please contact the college directly

Dr. Tammy Carter

****

Owmapow:

Bronx cheer right back at her! :-)

Rena

****

Rena:

The substitute position at the high school didn't work out (exaggerated raspberry sound). Doesn't anyone care if kids learn or not? I'd feel guilty if I just did the requested touchy-feely, "make the customers happy" stuff in the classroom.

Owmapow

****

Owmapow:

If they refused to fire you, it couldn't be THAT bad! C'mon! So, make them happy! Teach the way you want, while being part of their "joyful family!"

I didn't say to do only the touchy-feely! I said, "teach the way you want, but in a manner that pleases the administration." You shouldn't have to compromise on your principles! Just modify a bit. Make them AND you happy.

Any new acceptances of your fiction?

Rena

****

Rena:

They refused to fire me and, since I need the money, I refused to quit. However, they still insist that I change my behavior to conform to their "joyful family" model. Some folks are confused about their roles even after they grow up. Sigh. I'm not willing to compromise the insights into writing that I worked so hard to gain

No, only rejection notices.

Owmapow

****

Owmapow:

Uh Oh! This doesn't bode well! WHAT HAPPENED today? Did it go the way you expected or was it simply "another yucky day?" :-(

I hope you are smiling!

Rena

****

Rena:

At least there will always be lobsters.

Owmapow

Shredded Paper

Dear Owen Brownstone,

Thank you for filling out the Invertebrates Are Us questionnaire. We have received your response and will be issuing you a contract for the publication of your work, *Deep Water Creature Delights*. Congratulations! Your contract will be sent after Labor Day. Please confirm your mailing address.

To answer your question, our office is in New Orleans, but our distribution of books reaches many countries. Your idea of a release during the week of National Fishing Day could work.

Once again, congratulations from the Invertebrates Are Us family of publications.

Sincerely,
Carolyn DeSilva
Publisher
Invertebrates Are Us

****

Carolyn De Silvia:

Lo and behold! The contract arrived safely via snail mail. Looks good (it's boilerplate for small presses), except for one thing; I'm not okay with your clause of first right of refusal for my next book or next series of books.

Specifically, I work with different publishers for different genres. I'd be happy to amend that clause to read "first right of refusal for nonfiction anthologies about sea creatures," but not for all my works. *Crustaceans Never End* became an eBook through Paws Press and *Hedgehogs and Lobsters*, a poetry collection, has been shortlisted by Scales and Fins Ltd.

Per the genre, about which we are communicating, I have other manuscripts available (which I'm currently shopping them around), as well as one I'm developing. So, this counteroffer's not lame. Please let me know if my counteroffer suits you.

Meanwhile, ought I to ink in my changes on the contract, and then scan, and resend? Alternatively, should I wait for a redo of the paperwork from you?

I look forward to hearing from you. Have a nice Veterans' Day. I am glad to be welcomed into the Invertebrates Are Us family of publications.

Warm Wishes,
Owmapow
(Owen Brownstone)
P.O. Box 1248
Yellow Tide Road
Santa Barbara, CA 93160

****

Dear Owen, I Mean, Owmapow:

Per the publishing contract, just handwrite the change in the first right of refusal clause, initial it, make a copy, and include the copied page with your signature page when you send the contract back to me. First rights of refusal were not intended for every book, only for books in a series.

After you sign and send back the signature page and the page with
the change on it, please prepare a short bio and your author photo.
Then send them to me by e-mail. I will then post your photo and
bio. on the Invertebrates Are Us website.

I look forward to working with you. Happy Wintertime Holidays!

Sincerely,
Carolyn De Silvia

****

Carolyn:

Your specifics on how to amend the contract arrived the same day
as did my local animal rescue sanctuary's request for help with two
orphaned dugongs, so I'm only now getting back to a semblance of
sanity (semblance, for sure, given it's nearly 3 a.m. here and I am
still awake) and to you. I am sincerely sorry this response (along
with the rest of my professional life) got delayed.

I rewrote the clause as giving you first right of refusal, for six
months only, and only for *Estuary Creature Delights*, my next work
on important California fauna. Although not a series in the regular
sense, my books make for a hearty, contiguous read.

Others of my collections are under consideration at other houses.
ECD, too, was submitted to someone else, before I received
your contract but I'm willing to pull it from consideration, from
elsewhere, for half of a year. Ought I to do so?

There's likely a possibility for other offers from me, but let's
take these contracts one book at a time. My record is grand; I'm
beginning talks for a third book with one of my publishers and with
a different publisher for a second book.

Also, on my website, I made mention of our forthcoming project.
I have a LinkedIn page. I have a Facebook page, too (working with

you will motivate me to use it.) Shall I feature this book on those places, too?

Additionally, I have cover ideas when you're ready for such things. Speaking of which, please email to me a rough schedule for initial revised manuscript galley proofs, final proofs before printing, anticipated release date, etc. I have two other guppies lined up for a swim during the next few months and I am hoping to spend part of the summer teaching writing, so it's helpful to me to know your deadline expectations.

Anyway, my bio. is below. It will be updated when I have received countersigned contracts from a few other book publishers. Perhaps, I will also have more writing awards to add. In addition, if a certain teaching appointment comes through, I will also be able to amend my bio. To include "Distinguished Visiting Professor of Creative Writing." So, consider my bio. as a work in progress.

Four choices of photos are also below. I did a shoot of about 200 pix this summer. Note the oceanic backgrounds!

I will try to get to the post office, today, with the revised clause and signature pages. I will consider the contract valid when I receive your countersigned copy, especially your initials on the revised clause.

Hopefully, we will be able to create a few books together. I'm glad to join the Invertebrates Are Us family.

Warmly,
Owmapow

Current Bio:

Faithful in his devotion to the critters of the Santa Barbra Coast, Dr. Owen Brownstone researches *Decapoda*, specifically, and writes about ocean dwellers, in general. A biologist as well as a creative writer, his work can be found in: *Smarmy Friends, Under the Sea, Crazed Critters, Squeaks and Roars, Astral Flora and Fauna, Ocean*

Scavengers, Shellfish and Their Landlocked Buddies, and *Waving at Biology*! Dr. Brownstone spends his summers teaching science writing and creative nonfiction at the SBCC for Lifelong Learning.

****

Carolyn:

The contract was mailed yesterday. Sigh. A friend, who was helping me during my newest crisis with the dugongs, brought the papers to the post office, but inadvertently mailed the photocopy to you and returned the original to me. Please let me know when you receive the mailing. Once I receive your countersignatures on the specified pages, we will be legit.

Did my other email (author photos, etc.) make it to you? I look forward to working with you and Invertebrates Are Us Publishing.

Owen Brownstone

PS: when my book's production schedule becomes available, please send it to me.

****

Owen:

I need the original signature, not the copy. I received your photos and bio. They are great. When I receive the contract, the bio. and photo will be posted on the Invertebrates Are Us website. We have a Yahoo group for our authors, too. As soon as I receive your contract, I will send you the link. Happy George Washington's Birthday!

Sincerely,
Carolyn

****

Carolyn:

I was going to email you this week to ask if you had received the contract with its amendments. Not only was the original mailed to you, but a copy of the amended version was emailed, too. Can you work with electronic copies? Sigh. My local snail mail service is sometimes problem-ridden.

Meanwhile, my friend keeps trying to calm me down. She claims that all the copies will soon show up at your snail mailbox. She trusts the post office more than I do. Like me, she's a biologist. Her specialty, though, is *Theraphosinae*, so, few things bother her.

Many things, however, bother me, including the items I have permanently lost via snail mail. Never before have I had this problem when sending things to publishers. Then, again, the rest of my presses were fine with electronic mail.

I would like to get to this book's galley proofs. I await your reply.

Owmapow

****

Owmapow:

Thank-you for getting back to me. I have not had mail problems with other authors, but I have had personal issues with the post (even though, unlike your friend, I am not hardened by the study of tarantulas.)

If you sent multiple copies of the signed and amended contracts, one of them should show up. Let's give it a bit more time. I need an original signature, not an electronic one. I know that you are anxious about your work and your galleys, but we have a number of manuscripts ahead of yours, so the delay in my receiving your signature page will not have any impact on 'Invertebrates Are Us' release of your work.

Sincerely,
Carolyn

****

Carolyn:

Next month, I am due to present at the Aquaculture and Fisheries
Conference in Baton Rouge. When the conference concludes, if
my revised version of the contract has not yet arrived to you, I will
personally drive a fresh, signed copy to your office.

Owmapow

****

Dear Dr. Brownstone,

I have not received your signed contract. The policy of my company
is to have an original signature with the contract to countersign
and put the publishing agreement into force. We do not send our
contracts electronically. Unfortunately, your delay has caused some
bad news for you.

We have made a final decision. Since we don't believe such an
extensive delay would be fair to you, as it will create a missed
opportunity with another publisher, we are withdrawing our offer to
publish your work. We suggest that you submit *Deep Water Creature
Delights* to one of the other publishers with whom you work as the
manuscript is well written. We wish you the best of luck. Happy
Memorial Day

Sincerely,
Carolyn DeSilva
Publisher
Invertebrates Are Us

****

Ms. De Silvia:

Couldn't you wait a week until I arrive in Louisiana?

Owen Brownstone

****

Dear Owen,

As luck would have it, your paperwork in fact arrived the day after I had withdrawn the Invertebrates Are Us offer of a contract. Nonetheless, I won't be countersigning your papers. I wish you luck with your book.

Sincerely,
Carolyn

****

Carolyn:

I hold no grudges, except, against the postal service... I would still like to work on *Deep Water Creature Delights* with Invertebrates Are Us.

I'm glad the letter arrived. Thank-you for letting me know. I am very frustrated with the mail authority.

Owmapow

PS: My other book, *Estuary Creature Delights*, too, is still available.

****

Dear Owmapow:

I'm sorry but as per my prior email, I had withdrawn the contract, so I shredded the pages that you had sent. I don't keep contracts that I won't countersign. I care about protecting authors. I wish you luck with *Deep Water Creature Delights* and with *Estuary Creature Delights*. Have a nice Columbus Day!

Sincerely,
Carolyn DeSilva
Publisher
Invertebrates Are Us

Fame and Fortune

Dr. Owen Brownstone:

Thank you for sending us *Deep Water Creature Delights*. We love it and would like to include it in our publishing schedule for 2019. We will be in touch shortly with a contract.

Zilpa Jatkowitz
Publisher
Small Books and Bigger Objectives

****

Ms. Zilpa Jatkowitz:

Yee-haw! I can't wait to sign a contract with you! When will I receive it?

Dr. Owen Brownstone

****

Dr. Owen Brownstone:

I'm not yet sure when we're going to release *Deep Water Creature Delights*. Meanwhile, here's a copy of our boilerplate contract for your consideration.

Zilpa Jatkowitz

****

Ms. Zilpa Jatkowitz:

The contract looks good. Should I fill in the blanks and sign it? I'm more than okay with a publishing date that's over a year away. I have other projects in the works. I would, though, like to establish a manuscript due date for the rewrites of *Deep Water Creature Delights* so that I can adjust my calendar.

I look forward to hearing from you. Please don't hesitate to contact me!

Warmly,
Dr. Owen Brownstone

PS: Did I share with you that *Crazed Critter's* editor nominated one of my pieces, "Lobsters are Friends, not Food," for Best of the Net?

P^{2}S: PayPal suits me as a payment channel.

P^{3}S: Per copyright registration, do you know of an URL that gives step-by-step directions? (I think I need to take this action for others of my books, too.)

P^{4}S: Do you want an author photo for the back cover? When do you want a publicity biography? If this book is scheduled for the latter half of 2019, perhaps these items should wait as I might garner more awards/peer recognition in the interim.

P^{5}S: Please clarify;

"Author may use the cover art, or any other promotional artwork provided by Publisher for the Work in Author's own promotional material as long as this agreement is in force and at their own discretion."

vs

"Publisher will provide Author with digital formats of cover art, promotional art and advertising copy for the use of promoting the Work while this agreement is in force."

Does that mean I can use a jpg of the cover for my website? That I can use a jpg of the cover for my author interviews? Other?

****

Dr. Owen Brownstone:

Congratulations on your nomination! That's wonderful.

Yes, please fill in the contract.

Zilpa Jatkowitz

****

Ms. Zilpa Jatkowitz:

Thank-you for your warm wishes. I gush when folks say nice things about me (or nominate me for awards). Book contracts, too, make me smile.

Warmly,
Owmapow
(Dr. Owen Brownstone)

****

Dr. Owen/Owmapow:

Sorry for the delay. I've been swamped.

I'd like an author photo—it doesn't have to be fancy. It does, however, need to be hi-res. Fun/casual is fine. Yes, we can wait until next year. We're looking at November 2019, so if you win the Ocean Discovery XPrize, you have plenty of time to update your biography.

Also, you can use the cover image wherever you like for promotion, while we're still publishing your book. Should we part ways, should you decide to self-publish, or should you go with another publisher, you'll have to get a new cover.

I'll be *Deep Water Creature Delights'* project editor. I tend to run three to four rounds of edits and two rounds of proofing. The first edit will be for content. Later, a finer copy edit will be done by another staff member. Thereafter, yet another employee and you will proof the final document. We'll send you a PDF as well as a print copy to proof.

I'll ask you to provide some information about yourself to help market the book. I need websites, social networking links, your bio., your bibliography, a head shot, etc.

A few months before *Deep Water Creature Delights'* release, our Art Director, Ronald Kendell, will contact you with his draft of the cover art. He'll also ask you about the variety of graphic content you'll need for cards, banners, and bookmarks.

At about the same time, our PR intern, Nancy May, will likewise contact you about promoting *Deep Water Creature Delights* and about branding yourself as an author. Finally, Small Books and Bigger Objectives will provide you with a zip file of the eBook in PDF, ePub, and Mobi forms, all of which you can share with friends, colleagues, and book reviewers.

I've attached the completed contract. Thank-you for filling in the missing data. Please print, sign, and return the contract to me. The best method is for you to scan and to email me the signature page. I'm looking forward to working with you. Again, I apologize for the delay.

Zilpa Jatkowitz

****

Zilpa:

The signed signature page is attached. May I announce this project? I'm so excited about *Deep Water Creature Delights*!

Nov. 2019 suits me. When will I receive your first round of editing requests? What is the temporal spacing among the three or four rounds of edits?

When do you want author info? Hopefully, I'll have more good news in the coming year. I'm not sure about the Ocean Discovery XPrize, but an oceanographer can dream. This past week, *Shellfish and Their Landlocked Buddies* ran a longish author interview of me. Later this month, one of my electronic chapbooks, *Shells' Bells*, will get produced. I think, otherwise, you are up to date on my relevant comings and goings. Just let me know when you want me to package these data and which bits you want me to include/exclude.

When do you need the photo? I have a photographer I'd like to use, but I'd rather shoot closer to the release date than now, if possible.

I am looking forward to working with you, too! No worries about delays. All good things are worth waiting for ;) What's more, I appreciate your editing rigor. I'm having good premonitions about your marketing, too. I am sincerely glad you are going to be the publisher of *Deep Water Creature Delights*. Please let me know when I will hear from you.

Warmly,
Owmapow

****

Dear Owen/Owmapow:

I have this niggling suspicion that we were supposed to Skype last month. Was that my bad?

Let me know, because we're still interested in *Deep Water Creature Delights*.

Sincerely, and With Apologies,
Zilpa Jatkowitz

****

Zilpa:

Maybe, my bad. I was getting so worried about *Deep Water Creature Delights*, i.e., about receiving your countersignature on the contract, that I also offered the book to Invertebrates Are Us, LLC. Fortunately for Small Books and Bigger Objectives, my union with Invertebrates Are Us was not meant to be.

Regardless of book contracts, I've been working through a crisis with dugongs, so I have not read weeks' worth of emails, FB messages, Skype notices, or whatnot. Please forgive if it was me who dropped the ball (I even asked another publisher to wait a month to send me proofs for a book I'm launching with them.) No one explains, in attachment parenting manuals, about how to release children into the world. I will miss the dugongs.

Fortunately, writing is more of a fluid experience than is creature rearing. Acceptances keep coming in! My life, with all its glorious poignancy, seems to make for good copy. I'm sure it wouldn't surprise you to know that one of the works I poked at today was a poem called "Fins in the Wake" and that another was an essay entitled "Sometimes, Extra Fermentation: Seaweed's Medicinal Uses."

What if we Skyped sometime next week? As well, pronto, I need your signature on our contract.

Also, I have some questions about paperwork. I notice that you are Greek yet living in Ireland. Although your business address is

Athens, where do you file tax documents? Will it matter that I am an American author?

Further, what sort of editing schedule are you envisioning? My calendar is filling up.

Warmly,
Owmapow

****

Dear Owen/Owmapow:

Whew! What a relief! Let's Skype on Sunday, 16:00 GMT +0 okay?

Meanwhile, go ahead and announce. Honestly, it's a bit far in advance for me to have a production schedule. My waiting for your author picture is fine, as well as is my waiting for your bio. Per the bio, please send something personal rather than a list of awards, credits, and accomplishments. The key to sales is engagement with readers; writers need to show their human side. Readers want to buy books from writers who narrate about the human experience. As such, some of Small Books and Bigger Objectives' best sellers are by authors with no prior publication credits. People pay for marvelous storytellers regardless of their credentials.

Zilpa Jatkowitz

****

Zilpa:

Super! Do you mind if I begin additional rewrites this month, before hearing from you or ought I to wait to see which points are the most important to you? I realize that manuscripts can go through literally dozens of redos before they are market-ready.

As per persona, I'd like to keep to the "brand" that I've established thus far of being a biologist who writes about ocean dwellers. Just let me know what sort of "music" you enjoy, and if it is in a key I know, I'll be happy to dance to it.

Further, I think we are seven hours different in time zones. Accordingly, four in the afternoon in Dublin would be nine in the morning in California. Would an evening meeting suit you? If you called me at seven in the morning, your time, it would be midnight, here, which would suit me better than your originally proposed time.

Warmly,
Owmapow

PS: I still need your countersignature on the contract.

****

Owen:

The temporary book cover is up, but it doesn't reflect the intended audience for your book. Now that I understand that *Deep Water Creature Delights* isn't a collection of short stories, but a collection of scholarly essays, I think we need to rethink the project from cover to author bio., to marketing slant, and so forth.

Here's what I have, so far;

In this important book about crustaceans, Dr. Owen Brownstone brings us along on boudoir adventures. We join him in touring Pacific seabeds, where *Pleuroncodes planipes*, i.e., red crabs, and *Ostracods*, i.e., seed shrimp, breed. He takes us, too, to California lagoons, where *Aplysia californica*, California sea hares, fornicate with abandon. Readers are equally able to experience the fertility rituals of *Tagelus californianus*, California jackknife clams.

I realize that your writing is "experimental," but I think *Deep Water Creature Delights'* description should be clearer. Keep in mind that most readers lack your Ph.D. Keep in mind, too, that I have NOT yet read your entire manuscript.

Also, your author bio. is lackluster. What you sent me was;

Faithful in his devotion to the critters of the Santa Barbra Coast, Dr. Owen Brownstone researches *Decapoda*, specifically, and writes about ocean dwellers, in general. A biologist as well as a creative writer, his work can be found in: *Smarmy Friends, Under the Sea, Crazed Critters, Squeaks and Roars, Astral Flora and Fauna, Ocean Scavengers, Shellfish and Their Landlocked Buddies*, and *Waving at Biology*. Dr. Brownstone spends his summers teaching science writing and creative nonfiction at the SBCC Center for Lifelong Learning.

We need to jazz you up. Do you have children? A lover? Goldfish? Do you taxidermy sea critters?

Try to get the changes for your book description and your bio. to me by March.

Regards,
Zilpa Jatkowitz

****

Zilpa:

Attached, please find a mock-up of my montage idea for *Deep Water Creature Delights'* cover. Note the glorious *Cerithidea californica*, California horn snails, in the lower right quadrant.

As well, here's a revised book description;

Exoskeleton-bearing aquatic invertebrates are the new sexy. Tag along with Dr. Owen Brownstone as he gets up close and personal with crustaceans, bivalves, and molluscs. Learn the mating habits of red crabs, seed shrimp, and jackknife clams. Your bedroom partners will be glad you did.

Here's a revised author biography;

Like Dr. Laura Whitfield, Dr. Owen Brownstone believes in the space lobsters of Mars. Until he can afford his own rocket, however, he limits his research to California estuaries and to deep water breeding grounds off the western coast. A biologist as well as a creative writer, his work can be found in: *Smarmy Friends*, *Under the Sea*, *Crazed Critters*, *Squeaks and Roars*, *Astral Flora and Fauna*, *Ocean Scavengers*, *Shellfish and Their Landlocked Buddies*, and *Waving at Biology*! Dr. Brownstone owns no goldfish but has a special fondness for dugongs.

Warmly,
Owmapow

PS: our contract's still missing your countersignature!

****

Owen:

I'm sorry for the terribly long delay. I want to discuss a few things with you. Due to economic circumstance, Small Books and Bigger Objectives has decided, effective immediately, to produce all releases in digital form before issuing them in print. We need to reduce our fiduciary outlay.

If you would prefer to withdraw *Deep Water Creature Delights* because of these changes, I would understand. I'd even provide my endorsement of the project. If, on the other hand, you are willing to go with digital publication first, then Small Books and Bigger Objectives would still like to have *Deep Water Creature Delights* on our list.

Please let me know. Our policy changes are no reflection on your work. Thanks for your understanding.

Zilpa Jatkowitz
Publisher
Small Books and Bigger Objectives

****

Zilpa:

I am happy with the edits I have made so far to *Deep Water Creature Delights*. I plan to keep editing and to get the next redo to you by March. I hope we can still have a Nov. launch.

I've given a lot of thought to what you said about going digital. In Dec., I had a book of imaginings, *The Day Shellfish Took over the World*, go digital. Otherwise, all my books, except for *Crustaceans Never End*, began in print.

I don't want to withdraw *Deep Water Creature Delights* from your list. In fact, I don't want to part with Small Books and Bigger Objectives in any way, shape, or form. I want to stay friends, too.

On balance, I continue to believe that *Deep Water Creature Delights* has the potential to increase my attraction to readers. Accordingly, I have an idea. Let's do a two eBook contract. Let's package the contract for *Deep Water Creature Delights* with a contract for *Estuary Creature Delights* (I have yet to find a publisher for the latter.)

Given my other writing commitments, I could finish editing *Estuary Creature Delights* as well as complete its front and end matters at about the same time as Small Books and Bigger Objectives launches *Deep Water Creature Delights*. I envision a mid 2020 launch for *Estuary Creature Delights*.

If I could look to a two book contract with you, your change in house policy could work for me as I could better establish myself as an eBook writer. Let me know what you think about this idea.

Owmapow

****

Dr. Owen Brownstone:

There really isn't any difference between writing for eBooks and writing for print other than the use of paper. If you decide to stay with us, *Deep Water Creature Delights* will be placed in the digital market and then re-evaluated every ninety days for possible print publication.

We aren't really going to be adding any more science treaties to our schedule at present. So, I'm going to have to respectfully decline your offer of a 2-book deal.

Zilpa Jatkowitz
Publisher
Small Books and Bigger Objectives

****

Zilpa:

Maybe we can put our creative heads together and think of something else.

Warmly,
Owmapow

PS: No matter what we do, I still need your countersignature!

****

Dr. Owen Brownstone:

All Small Books and Bigger Objectives' forthcoming titles will be initially released in digital form and then re-evaluated every ninety days for possible print release. We honestly are not interested in any more science treaties. These policies have nothing to do with your work and everything to do with our resources.

Zilpa Jatkowitz
Publisher
Small Books and Bigger Objectives

****

Zilpa:

I am sincerely sorry to hear about your company's challenges. Sigh. The publishing industry is anything but stable.

I've talked to a friend. I need to graciously take your offer to leave behind our contract. Shucks! I had looked forward to doing business with Small Books and Bigger Objectives. Writers, too, even midlist ones, like me, must protect themselves.

The electronic chapbook that I've offered for free, *The Day Shellfish Took over the World*, was my nod toward a Creative Commons' distribution of my ideas. I've already tried one full-length, electronic book release, *Crustaceans Never End*, with poor results. For now, I need at least a "for fee" POD level of distribution for my work.

Please send me whatever forms I need to sign. I want to make sure we properly complete closure on *Deep Water Creature Delights*.

I sincerely wish you and Small Books and Bigger Objectives the best of all profit and publicity. I've enjoyed our relationship.

Sincerely,
Owmapow

PS: I no longer need your countersignature.

Owmapow Keeps Trying

Hi Jeremy!

When I read that your uncle died, I thought about you, about Sam, and about Betty. I know that you, and my cousin Liam, are still friends.

I've long thought of you as Liam's pal as much as I've thought of you as Sam's little brother. (Liam hates it when I speak of him as "my little cousin" as he's fifty, after all. Nonetheless, some habits don't fade as readily as do others.)

Anyway, I still have, somewhere, pictures of you and Liam from a birthday party. I could look for that photo album, scan it, and email it to you, if you would like. Regardless, you'd probably be pleased had you been aware that, intermittently, I sent you regards through Liam.

Per Sam, your brother, when I was a confused middle schooler, Sam was one of the most benevolent kids I knew. He never made fun of my pet fish, turtles, and snails, and never mocked my interest in oceanography. He never teased me for trading baseball cards for critters, either.

As per Betty, I only knew her as "Sam and Jeremy's sister." Sorry.

Anyway, I wanted to get in touch with Sam to wish him my condolences, so I googled him. Nada.

After graduate school, I essentially lost touch with everyone from childhood. Thus, I didn't know if he had become more private or, maybe, took up a religion that caused him to change his name. If it's okay with him, would you forward his email address to me?

I googled your sister. It seems she's settled and happy. I wish her all the best.

I googled you. You're an agent! You're Liam's age. You are no longer my little sister's equally young friend's younger brother, but someone who climbed the rungs of the publishing industry! Wow! Meanwhile, you've kept that great smile you had when we were kids.

As for me, I stayed in California after school, became a biology professor, and taught science writing on the side.

Anyway, I am taking a risk with the next sentence, with a request. Can I pitch *Estuary Creature Delights* to you? I've attached a tease (not an actual synopsis).

When might you be game to read more? I've had the fortune to meet all sorts of publishers, editors, agents, and writers in the last few years. However, I'd rather talk to you than to a stranger. I hope my boldness is not off-putting.

The above, aside, I'm sending you my condolences per your uncle. Please ask Sam if I can have his email address.

Warmly,
Owmapow (Owen Brownstone)

****

Owen:

Thank you for your thoughtful condolences and for your lovely memories. There is much to which to respond, but it may take me a few weeks as I am playing catch up after a lot of business travel and bereavement. I did however want to connect with you with Sam, who I know would enjoy a hello (he's cc'd above.)

Jeremy

****

Jeremy:

Thank-you for Sam's address!! I'm going to drop him a quick email before I'm off to sleep.

Owmapow

****

Hi Jeremy!

I. am. so. grateful. to. be. reconnected. to. Sam!!!!!!! Thanks! (Your brother is just as wonderful as he was when we were kids. I look forward to an ongoing, email relationship with him.)

In other matters, may I pitch *Estuary Creature Delights* to you? Please advise. Also, sometime in the future, I want to publish a second edition of my poetry assemblage, *Hedgehogs and Lobsters*. Might you be interested in representing a reprint of this collection?

PS: Some of my freestanding work includes: "Crustaceans in Deep Space," in *Astral Flora and Fauna*, "The Care and Feeding of Rabid Hedgehogs" in *Smarmy Friends*, "The Elephant's Toe" in *Crazed Critters*, and "Squamata's Big Dance" in *Squeaks and Roars*.

The herbs are flowering. The otters are mating. Life is good.

I Await Your Email!

Owmapow

****

Hi Owen:

I'm heading off to vacation and am focusing on doing nothing professional for a few weeks. This is just a quick note to say I'm glad you and Sam reconnected.

All the Best,
Jeremy

****

Hi Owmapow

Whereas Jeremy Hudson is beloved to us, no agent can restructure the market. So, knowing him is no help to you, at present.

Aiden Pullela
Managing Editor
Sebastian Press

****

Hi Owmapow,

I can draft up a formal release of contract, but let this notice serve until then that we both agree to release each other from the contract with no contingencies. Thanks for your understanding. I wish things were different, but our press needs to pare down so that we don't have to close our door.

Aiden Pullela
Managing Editor
Sebastian Press

****

Aiden:

I found myself on your mailing list for "Help us Promote Your Books on Facebook." I'm glad to see your publishing house is back on the track and is again offering new books in print and digital forms. To wit, I'd love for you to honor your contract with me for *Estuary Creature Delights*.

You asked me to release you from the contract since you thought I ought to publish not only digitally, but also in print. I released you. In the interim, I signed contracts for other books, but not for that one.

Now, from the email, I see you are again offering print products. How can we return to our commitment?

Owmapow

****

Hi Owmapow,

I'm sorry about the email mix-up. We are still producing only limited print copies and are only publishing in specific genres at present. But thanks for keeping touch.

Aiden Pullela
Managing Editor
Sebastian Press

****

Aiden:

We had a contract. I sent you a 70,000 word book, *Estuary Creature Delights*, for which you have yet to formally revoke our contract. Meanwhile, your list of new releases, as provided at http://www. Sebastianpress.com, includes print and electronic releases of new titles.

I don't feel good about this discovery. Perhaps, a year ago, your press was short funded. This year, however, you seem to be *printing* plenty of books. Since I would like to work with you, I am going to suppose that we have a misunderstanding.

Owmapow

PS: On second thoughts, I don't want to publish where I'm not appreciated. I hope you succeed with your press. Consider this email notice that I'm submitting *Estuary Creature Delights* elsewhere.

Coffee Shop Crush

Dear Dr. Sylvia Anucha:

Please don't think I'm stalking you or am otherwise weird. Simply, I saw you in the student union coffee shop, sipping what might have been a latte, and was smitten by your auburn hair. I realized I've seen you on campus, so I looked up your profile on the faculty pages of our college of science's website. I'm glad our university categorizes faculty by their respective colleges.

Anyway, you're far prettier than that blond mathematician, Kayla Morton. Plus, you have more charm than that physics professor, Anna Wu.

Whereas it might seem old school for me to contact you via email, before seeking you in person, at least I'm not employing a carrier pigeon or a singing telegram. Maybe, you'll consider my mode of communication somewhat contemporary, nonetheless.

Feel free to search for me in our college of science's faculty directory. You will discover that I am an Associate Professor of Biology and that I have been faithfully serving our university for thirteen years. Prior, I worked at another school for thirty years.

My hobbies include teaching science writing and writing science fiction, two diametrically polar pursuits, albeit both of which make me happy. I adore critters, words, and words about critters.

Unfortunately, I've remained a bachelor, having had more success aiding *Ostracods*, seed shrimp, and *Aplysia californica*, California sea hares, with breeding than mixing and mingling with my own species. So, I'm inviting you to have your next student union coffee on my tab, in my company.

I'm no creep, hence, I am suggesting a very public place. At worst, you'll spend a quarter of an hour with someone who would love to discuss biology with you. I noticed that your specialty is using neural nets to combine large numbers of cryo-EM images to demonstrate the range of three-dimensional configurations of protein complexes. Fascinating work! I wished you were housed in my department so that I might have gotten to meet you earlier. However, it's to the Computational Systems Department's credit that you're housed with them.

I suppose that you know that snacking in the student union sometimes leads to having to interact with students. I find complaints about midterm lab grades to be the most annoying of those interactions, but I temper my responses by remembering how I felt when I was an undergraduate. My parents wanted me to be a doctor. I wanted to be an oceanographer. You can deduce who won.

Hopefully Yours in Friendship,
Dr. Owen Brownstone

****

Dr. Owen Brownstone:

Thank-you for your caring words. I'm not in the market for a suitor, but I'm always glad to have a new friend. However, I would appreciate it if you were more careful in how you referred to people. Both Kayla and Anna are friends of mine.

In fact, the three of us are this city's committee for STEM outreach to high school girls. Unfortunately, at present, girls, even those who have little trouble in identifying as mathematically gifted, are put off, due to familial, peer, and broader social pressures, from pursuing sciences and applied sciences.

The three of us discourse on many topics, as "experts." Sadly, though, none of us are engineers. If Molly Zagstan, who is currently an Assistant Professor of Mechanical Engineering, and who is focused on micro devices used in energy systems, receives tenure, maybe, she'll join our ranks. Likewise, if Risa Habtu, Assistant Professor of Artificial Intelligence, whose specialty is natural language processing, receives tenure, she, too, would be a welcomed addition to our task force.

No matter. When I googled you, I saw that you had some fiction published, e.g., "The Care and Feeding of Rabid Hedgehogs," in *Smarmy Friend*, and "The Elephant's Toe," in *Crazed Critters*. but did not have many peer review journal articles. I would have expected to see your research written up in *ICES Journal of Marine Science, Marine Policy*, or *The Journal of Marine Research*. I don't think that your blogs for *Shellfish and Their Landlocked Buddies* or your posts in the children's site, *Under the Sea*, count. How did you earn your tenure?

Sylvia Anucha

****

Sylvia Anucha:

Creative writing has become dear to me. My sister, Dr. Rachel Brownstone, of Brown University, though younger, is savvy about all things involving people. She taught me how to understand my audience, that is, how to grasp the gist of what my tenure and promotion committee was seeking, and how to focus my energies on getting published in the journals that are most esteemed by them. If you look under my picture on our university website, you'll note that my research has also appeared in *Astral Flora and Fauna, Ocean Scavengers*, and *Waving at Biology*. My committee deemed that I was a star in public outreach and tenured me under a public education clause.

Owen

****

Owen:

Is your sister a lady of science? I'm doubting that fact as I see the words "rhetoric" and "communication" associated with her name. If I am mistaken about her academic contributions, even though I checked the internal consistency of my hypothesis twice, maybe she can start a STEM chapter for high school girls at her university.

Sylvia

****

Sylvia:

She's a humanist, or, at best, a social scientist.

Regardless, what does it mean to be your "friend?" I'm rather busy maintaining my tanks of *Tagelus californianus*, California jackknife clams and hatching my Pacific Lampreys. I used to raise dugongs, too.

On a different topic, did you know that obesity is more common in large amphibians, such as the South American Horned Frogs, the Barred Tiger Salamander, and the Eastern Tiger Salamander, than in small ones such as microhylid frogs, the Virgin Islands Dwarf Gecko, and the Mount d'Ambre Leaf Chameleon? Critters in captivity have lower energy needs than do feral ones and most captive animals are the smallest of their respective classes.

Maybe, I should mentor zoos and pet shops. It's a pity that so many of the animals that are under human care sicken and die from too much food.

Owen

****

Owen:

For starts, a friend is sensitive toward, i.e., does not insult another friend. I can't believe that you had the audacity to suggest that I am overweight, explicitly, or even to suggest, more universally, that my appearance matters. Are there no men who are not chauvinists?

My third husband mocked me for my respiratory challenges, my visible excessive bulk, and my alleged difficulty moving. He even had the audacity to suggest that I was lethargic despite my publication record and my membership in our university's beach volleyball league. It was so easy to divorce him when he was offered that deanship at Vassar College. Nevertheless, I can't believe that the school hired such a woman-hater!

Dr. S. Anucha

****

Dr. Sylvia Anucha:

I'm confused as to what my concern for the well-being of ocean and estuary creatures has to do with your personal life. Next, you'll blame me for the glasses perched on your nose or for your widow's peak. Sheesh!

Perhaps, we ought not to correspond. Initially, I had hoped to date you. Thereafter, I was glad to be considered as a candidate for your friendship. At the moment, though, I'm not sure any association between us is wise.

Dr. Owen Brownstone

****

Dr. Brownstone:

You can make whatever assumptions you like. I've already

forwarded copies of our electronic correspondence to the head of our school's Human Resources Department. Expect a summons.

Dr. Sylvia Anucha

****

Dr. Sylvia Anucha:

Maybe, you could retract your complaint? I'm just an oceanographer who espied a pretty redhead in the student union coffee shop. I'm fine without any further connection to you. However, I'm not fine being labeled a gender bigot as I admired, not despised, or minimalized, you.

My sister, Dr. Rachel Brownstone, suggests that I apologize for my linguistic oversights and that I offer to buy you, strictly as a peer, a cup of coffee. Might we mend fences? I'm good with webbed, finned, and scaly critters, not with humans and their many nuances.

Dr. Owen Brownstone

****

Dr. ~~Brownstone~~ Owen:

In truth, you're kind of cute, in an awkward way. My second husband accused me of harpy-like behavior. I certainly don't want to be referred to as "cruel" or as "grasping." I reported you on principle, not due to circumstances. You oughtn't to call women "webbed," "finned," or "scaly."

Regardless, I accept your offer of a cup of coffee in that very public venue. The beans, there, are not fresh, but the shop's just a five minute walk from my office.

Dr. Sylvia

****

Dr. Sylvia:

If we're going to try to be friends, maybe you would consider dropping those charges? In another year, I'm applying for a promotion to Full Professor. I think having a "record of incitement" will work against my best interests.

Dr. Owen

****

Owen:

Unlike my other husbands, my first, a green card-seeking graduate student from Croatia, never said I was too physically luscious or too vocally able. We parted only after he met and wanted to wed, that is to marry for love, a transfer student from Albania. Ironically, it was the green card that our union had bestowed upon him that enabled him to marry that little girl. Since the entire ten thousand dollars, which was her wedding gift to him, was transferred to my bank account, we parted amicably.

My point is, I like men. I just don't like how they treat me. Maybe, I overreacted a bit to our emails. Kayla says I should retract my complaint. Anna says I should leave it be and try dating women. Kayla wins as I'm a through and through a heterosexual.

Please don't trim your hair before we get coffee. I really like your sloppy bangs.

Sylvia

****

Sylvia:

Thank-you for meeting me for coffee. That green sweater looked nice. I am, anyway, confused. Do you want to be my friend? Do you want to date? Will you retract that complaint that you made against me? I thought you had already done so, but you said, while sipping that mud, that you had not.

Owen

****

Owen:

It's my experience that it's better to be friends than lovers, even if you are a man and I'm attracted to men. Thanks, by the way, for not trimming your bangs.

Sylvia

****

Sylvia:

My sister thinks you're objectifying me. That's not misogyny, but misandry. It's not nice.

Owen

****

Owen:

Our exchanges are growing tiresome. I think you should spend more time researching Humboldt Squid or writing about ocean scavengers rather than trying to establish relationships with members of the fair sex.

Sylvia

****

Sylvia:

I think you're right. I'd have better luck trying to get anadromous fish to breed than wrangling an actual date with you. It's a pity. You're as attractive as a beach at low tide and as smart as a Goby.

Owen

****

Dr. Brownstone:

Your last email reminded me of why it was wise for me not to drop my complaint against you. It remains on file at Human Resources. Furthermore, I won't be too sorry if it adversely impacts your promotion. After all, you made "nice nice" to me by hosting me for a cup of horrible coffee and then had the nerve to compare me to a whale!

I don't like women, yet I can't help but believe that men will always be cretins. All of you are stupid, vulgar, and insensitive.

Have a Good Life,
Dr. Sylvia Anucha

****

Dr. Anucha:

I have almost half of a dozen witnesses who are willing to testify seeing you drip liquified henbane into my cuttlefishes' tank. You, too, now have a file... at the city's police station.

Disappointed in Love,
Dr. Owen Brownstone

Owmapow Rides Again

Hi Owen!

I am an editor for the oceanic line at The Harsh Earth Press. As such, I will be the reviewing editor for your book. I have to say, it sounds like a refreshing change from all the author-writing-in-coffee shop stories that have come in lately. I will be back to you within three weeks.

Effie
Effie Jones
www.TheHarshEarth.com

****

Dear Dr. Brownstone,

Thank you for your interest in The Harsh Earth Press. Effie Jones passed your file to me. I read your query. I invite you to submit the entire manuscript of *Estuary Creature Delights*. Feel free to shoot me an email if you have any questions.

Have a great day!

Lara Sánchez
Senior Editor, Oceanic Earth
The Harsh Earth Press, Inc.

****

Effie:

I hope you and Lara Sánchez are sufficiently refreshed enough to vote "yes!" Please feel free to swim any questions you have about my project to me.

Warmly,
Owmapow
(Dr. Owen Brownstone)

****

Owmapow:

I reformatted your manuscript to make it easier for us to work with since you have an extra space between each paragraph. Please eliminate those spaces manually and then return your work to us.

Lara Sánchez
Senior Editor, Oceanic Earth
The Harsh Earth Press, Inc.

****

Lara:

I am confused. Do you want me to enjamb the paragraphs? Do you want me to change the spacing from 1.5 lines to 1 line, too? Other?

Owmapow

****

Owmapow:

The line spacing is fine. You added paragraph spaces between each paragraph, though—not fine.

You never heard the word "enjamb?" It means "to put the paragraphs together like in a real book." I thought you were a professor.

Lara Sánchez
Senior Editor, Oceanic Earth
The Harsh Earth Press, Inc.

****

Lara:

I'm still confused. I ran the text through Word's paragraph spacing doohickie and verified that there is no "extra" space among paragraphs. There's just the 1.5 lines between the end of one paragraph and the beginning of another. That's the same amount of space as there is among lines in the paragraphs.

Besides being a biology professor, I'm a published writer. Did you read any of my freestanding works, such as Crustaceans in Deep Space," in *Astral Flora and Fauna*, "The Care and Feeding of Rabid Hedgehogs" in *Smarmy Friends*, "The Elephant's Toe" in *Crazed Critters*, or "Squamata's Big Dance" in *Squeaks and Roars*?

Owmapow

****

Owmapow:

If you turn on Word's paragraphing icon, you can see it. They show up as paragraph symbols. You know, the backwards "P."

Lara Sánchez
Senior Editor, Oceanic Earth
The Harsh Earth Press, Inc.

****

Lara:

I attached a sample page of what I think you are asking for. Please tell me if this is the format you want.

Owmapow

****

Owmapow:

That's exactly right. I don't mean to be a pain but it's the way ALL publishers want to receive manuscripts. Also, IF we go any further, your manuscript will have to be put into this format. AND if I send it to the reading team, they, too, will need the proper format.

Lara Sánchez
Senior Editor, Oceanic Earth
The Harsh Earth Press, Inc.

****

Lara:

Phew! Done! Attached. Please let me know if you need anything else.

Owmapow

****

Owmapow:

I really enjoy your voice—it's unique and quirky. I want to send it to the reading team for their evaluation. Meanwhile, there are numerous issues with punctuation as well as some typos. One thing is there isn't any dialogue. Could you give your manuscript a serious going-over? The manuscript needs to be in the best possible condition when it goes to the reading team, which means it needs its punctuation fixed.

Lara Sánchez
Senior Editor, Oceanic Earth
The Harsh Earth Press, Inc.

****

Lara:

No problem. I'll be able to have a redo done in a week or so (I'm currently in the midst of another project). Would that be okay?

Owmapow

****

Owmapow:

Whatever works for you. I'm sorry to keep sending your manuscript back, but I want to give it the best shot with the reading team.

Lara Sánchez
Senior Editor, Oceanic Earth
The Harsh Earth Press, Inc.

****

Lara:

Redone, again. Phew! Attached.

Owmapow

****

Owmapow:

I read your book, once more, and realized that your diction is not fit for the average reader—a requirement of the Oceanic Line, so I sent it to the Academic Line's editor for her to see if it belongs with her. I'll be in touch.

Lara Sánchez
Senior Editor, Oceanic Earth
The Harsh Earth Press, Inc.

****

Owmapow:

I'm sorry, while your book is too scholarly for the line I edit, it's likewise insufficiently grounded in peer reviewed work for our Academic Line. Thank-you for thinking of The Harsh Earth Press.

Lara Sánchez
Senior Editor, Oceanic Earth
The Harsh Earth Press, Inc.

Dogged Dr. Brownstone

Dr. Phillip Bryn:

I need to withdraw *Deep Water Creature Delights* from offer. Another small press will be publishing it. In its place, might I offer you *Estuary Creature Delights*?

Warmly,
Dr. Owen Brownstone
(Owmapow)

****

Dr. Brownstone:

I will happily accept your second book, *Estuary Creature Delights*. Meanwhile, congratulations on *Deep Water Creature Delights*. Let's mention that book on your author page.

However, since I have four more books to release this year, I'm waiting until January to contract my next titles. As well, one of my most annoying authors stole artwork, so I need to terminate his project. Sigh. Also, redesigning Smells Fishy Publishing's website sent me scuttling, but I think that having an easier-to-access portal is worth the concomitant pain. For sure, it's never boring here.

Sincerely,
Phillip Bryn

****

Hi Phillip Bryn:

I'm thrilled that you have accepted *Estuary Creature Delights*. I look forward to receiving a contract from you in January. Meanwhile, I'll send letters, to promote our forthcoming book, to venues that published my short works; *Astral Flora and Fauna, Smarmy Friends, Crazed Critters,* and *Squeaks and Roars*. Additionally, please find attached pictures of *Rhithropanopeus harrisii*, Harris mud crabs, and of *Ostrea lurida*, Olympia oysters, as possible front and back cover images for *Estuary Creature Delights*.

Sincerely,
Owmapow

****

Dr. Bryn:

Maybe your computer is eating my email. Please, by the end of this week, either tell me you are no longer interested in my books or send me the promised contract for *Estuary Creature Delights*. I'd rather hear from you directly than resort to pulling my offer for lack of communication. Months ago, you promised I'd receive a contract in January and it's currently May. Ought I to send this project elsewhere?

Sincerely,
Owmapow

****

Dr. Bryn:

I hope the reason that I have had no response from you is because of something stupid I did and not, G-d forbid, because you, or a family member of yours, is in a dire place. I am guessing you are okay since Smells Fishy Publishing is still posting.

Whereas I hate leaving you, I do have to move forward. Hence, please consider this email my withdrawal of my offer to work with Smells Fishy Publishing on *Estuary Creature Delights*. Someday, perhaps, you will let me know why you stopped answering my emails.

Owmapow

****

Owmapow:

My dear writer, there is nothing you could do that would make me disregard your work. I am answering you on the fly between appointments because I do not want you to think that my too delayed response is because of anything wrong done by you. Truth be told, I have not caught up on issuing contracts because I have been overwhelmed.

Meaning, I've only managed one book release, so far, this year. I have tons of correspondence to catch up on, yours and others. I don't know whether you will find my words consoling or evidence of incompetence on my part.

I remain committed to publishing *Estuary Creature Delights*. I don't blame you for wanting to send it elsewhere, but I will get the contract to you by this summer. In fact, I'll jump your papers ahead of all the other books that are awaiting contracts.

Sincerely,
Phillip Bryn

****

Dr. Bryn:

I am confused. Are we contracting or not for *Estuary Creature*

Delights? Even the graduate students who help at my lab asked if I had received a contract, yet. They were disappointed with my "no."

If Smells Fishy Publishing can't/won't come forward with a contract, that's fine—just tell me. I just want closure. In the interim, I accepted a job supervising the docents at Santa Barbara's Museum of Natural History's shark touch pools, tidepool tank, and sea specimen exhibits.

My writing time, consequently, has dropped to almost nothing. I respect Smells Fishy Publishing, but I need straight communication so I can make plans. Please let me know what's going on with my contract.

Additionally, I've received a contract from another publisher for another book, *River Creature Delights.* That agreement is signed, and counter signed. Production is scheduled.

Owmapow

****

Oh Phillip:

How I wish it was not your hardships that waylaid our communication. Per your last email, it seems as though you've been further busied with helping your secretary with legal issues and with sourcing medical care for your grandmother.

As per Yours Truly, I remain a work in progress. I've had too many demands and too few resources, so, I've given up teaching face-to-face writing workshops for a while—they were a time sink when it came to advertising them, collecting students' fees, and the like. Maybe, soon, I'll offer online courses. Also, I've stopped blogging. At first, blogging gave me experience and visibility. More recently, though, it gave me crummy remuneration, unnecessary pressure, and insomnia.

In reconfiguring, I'm emphasizing book-length projects. To wit, I'm going to spend the next span retooling a commercial book (I've already written dozens of versions of this thing, and, in fact, have roughly 500-600 pages to prune.) What's more, I have plans to actualize some cherished projects, including *Marine Madness*, a collection of my short fiction about endangered aquatic critters. The characters therein include a fin whale and a Steller sea lion. Intermittently, I've been proofing the galleys for *River Creature Delights*, signing a contract for *Mysteries of the Mud Holes*, and what-have-you.

Accordingly, per *Estuary Creature Delights*, while I admire you as a publisher, you've broken a lot of promises to me. If you send me the contract for *Estuary Creature Delights* by the end of the month, we're good to go; I can wait until early 2020 for a launch. Nonetheless, unless I receive that authoritative piece of paper and can sign it and send it back to you for a countersignature, I consider this matter unsettled and request that you release me from our agreement.

Sincerely,
Owmapow

****

Owmapow:

I am excited that you'v taken on projects like *Marine Madness* and *Mysteries of the Mud Holes*! You ought to work on books that matter to you. Good luck!

Phillip

PS: The contract for *Estuary Creature Delights* is attached.

****

Phillip:

Thank-you for finally sending me the contract. Let's target next month for galley proofs. Does that suit you? As well, let's do the interview (see attached) at the conservation Ezine, *Whaling Away.* That publication supports nonviolent solutions to ecological crises.

Owmapow

PS: I'm starting to upgrade my website. I intend to add music, to paste in new images, and to update my list of published work.

****

Phillip:

Are we still good to go? I will be "out of the office" during the last week of July/first week of August. Please send me the galley proofs *now* so I can do my part on this project with immediacy. I must attend to *Mysteries of the Mud Holes* when I return to work. This waiting and waiting is making me feel crazy.

Owmapow

****

Owmapow:

Layout will be August and you can deal with galley proofs, thereafter. I can't wait to see your reaction to our work. Meanwhile, let's compile a list of people from whom to request back cover blurbs. I still have your crab and oyster images. Did you take those photos? If not, do you have permission to use them?

Phillip

****

Phillip:

I took those photos. Do you want more so that we can fashion a montage instead of using a single image? I'll ask professional friends, i.e., editors who know my writing, to supply blurbs for our book. I'm assuming, thus, I can send them copies before we proof galleys.

Owmapow

****

Owmapow:

I changed the order of the narratives in the last section of *Estuary Creature Delights*; after "All of the Wisdom that is a Sea Snail's," I put "Bountiful Beach Buffet: Loving Seaweed, aka Algae," "Cup Corals Merit," and "The Harmony of Sea Otters." I thought the progression felt better moving from smaller to larger species than the reverse. When you see the layout, you'll know whether it feels right to you or not.

Also, I think I have a better idea for the book's cover, but I'll need a few more of your photos of aquatic beasts. I'm glad the photos you sent were taken by you—production costs will be reduced as a result. I think you'll like what I'm conceptualizing. I'll keep you posted!

Phillip

****

Phillip:

Per the cover, I'll send more photos. Per the galley proofs, I'm still waiting. It's October, Phillip!

Owmapow

****

Owmapow:

I've been through two rounds of revisions with the freelancer and am hoping to have cover options for you by next week. This freelancer is a graduate of Cavalier School of Design. I'm pleased with the direction he's taking.

What are you doing with *Deep Water Creature Delights*? Will you be traveling to promote it? Might you mention our book, too?

Did you finish revising *Mysteries of the Mud Holes*? Do you think that *Whaling Away* might still be willing to do that interview with us?

I'm so impressed with your doggedness. I will get those galley proofs to you by January. I'm sure we'll be able to launch your title in no less than two more years.

Phillip

Around, Once More, with Owmapow

Dear Dr. Middleton:

Are you still seeking a Science Writer?

Dr. Owen Brownstone

****

Dr. Owen Brownstone:

The position is almost taken, but I would be happy to talk with you upon receipt of your CV, if you send it ASAP.

Thanks,
Dr. Middleton

****

Dear Dr. Middleton:

I am writing in response to your email. Writing about pain in fish is well within my bailiwick. Working on a team focusing on pain treatments for pain in humans, by studying those treatments on *Danio rerio* and on *Oryzias latipes* is part of my academic interests. See: *Shellfish and Their Landlocked Buddies'* longish author interview of me.

After all, I'm happy "translating" the academy's complex ideas into language that is usable by the public. In addition, I am a National

Science Foundation Scholar and have taught science writing to community college students. I think you will find me intelligent, creative, and able. That is, I think you will find me well-suited to your needs.

Attached is a chronological CV. Please contact me if you or your institute needs any additional information. I look forward to hearing from you.

Sincerely,
Dr. Owen Brownstone
(Owmapow)

****

Hi Owmapow!

Your experience looks good. Did you ever write for peer-reviewed, scientific journals? If so, which ones? Did you ever write about pain research?

Dr. Middleton

****

Dr. Middleton:

A good (science) writer must be facile with language. Such an individual, given a rudimentary "taste" of a topic's jargon, and given adequate information about the demographics and psychographics of the audience to whom his or her data is meant to address, can construct discourse suitable for that audience's needs. More exactly, a good writer must possess and use classic writing skills.

To wit, over the last few decades, I have challenged myself to teach, to write and to publish in domains in which I am not formally trained. I could not refer to myself as a "skilled" writer if I failed to communicate outside of rigid topical constraints.

Consider that my NSF Fellowship was actualized at Eastern New Mexico University's Biology Department (a snippet of that work is attached), and that my most recent peer review publications focused on *Pleuroncodes planipes*, and on *Ostracods*. It's interesting and important for me to grasp, to organize, and to articulate many types of ideas. What's more, recently, I've returned to creative work, e.g., to penning another short story for *Smarmy Friends*, and to offering up new, humorous essays for *Under the Sea*.

In short, I morph myself to fit audiences' needs. Because I can flex around various concepts, I am a better resource for "translating" subject-specific ideas into general and specialized texts than is someone trained in a limited sector of science. A little reading and few well-placed questions rocket me to "warp speed" on technical projects.

In view of my method for writing for scientific communities, I offer the following definitions. By "peer review scientific journals," I assume you mean publications like: *ICES Journal of Marine Science, Marine Policy,* and *Journal of Marine Research.* By "research," I assume you mean "scientific (method-based) analyses, interpretations, and evaluations."

Beyond crafting the above definitions, if you want to see how I work, please send me a sample page and the specifics about where these ideas are meant to appear. I will finesse the text accordingly. Alternatively, you could send me some of your unedited findings and could prescribe for me the type of short summary that you would want me to construct concerning them. I'll take on either of the above tasks for a nominal fee. I think you will be pleased with my results.

The work that you have been engaged in on pain management is interesting to me as a science writer, as a critical thinker, and as a biologist. It is incumbent upon us experts, who have benefited from many years of education, to do our part to help reduce human misery.

I will make a good addition to your research team. I look forward to hearing from you.

Sincerely,
Owmapow

****

Owmapow:

I will hire you to freelance for one paper. You will need to read a lot about the issue to edit well and to suggest additions to its introduction and conclusion. If I give you a standard paper draft, say 5000 words, to revise, what would be your fee?

James Middleton

****

James:

5,000 words is roughly twenty manuscript pages, at 250 words/ page. Based on the industry norm of approximately $70.00/ hour, and on the industry average of about ten pages per hour, this project should take me about two hours and should cost you about $140.00. However, I will not charge you for the time it takes me to read and to integrate new data since the task you are assigning me is meant to showcase my editing skills, not my sharp learning curve.

Please keep in mind that science writing fees are higher than are science editing fees. We can negotiate future cost when you offer me the writing position. Similarly, salaried work is usually less expensive than is contract work, but salaried employment involves a different type of commitment from an employer than does contractual work. Let's discuss such matters later.

I look forward to receiving the writeup of the project. Please do not hesitate to contact me if you have any questions.

Owmapow

****

Dear James:

I await a copy of the manuscript. Please forward it to this email address at your first convenience.

Owmapow

PS: If my terms of payment are unacceptable, please advise. I am eager to begin this project.

****

Dear Owmapow:

I am not sure which manuscript to send you. Do you know more about analgesic or anxiolytic treatments? Do you have online access to journals, or do you need to use our library?

James

****

Dear James:

Whereas I'd rather not check "quantitative stuff," i.e., I'd rather not check equations, since I prefer to trust your scientists have already checked and rechecked your lab results, I do enjoy rolling around in qualitative ideas. Why don't you send me the manuscript that has the roughest edges?

Along with that document, please indicate: your intended

audience, your intended tone, and the qualities you like, e.g., well substantiated claims, and dislike, e.g., lack of parsimony, in similar publications. I will follow your lead per the nature of the piece at the same time as I edit its arrangement of ideas and development of concepts.

I look forward to hearing from you.

Sincerely,
Owmapow

PS: Per admittance to a library, I have entrée, through my own department, to many journals. However, if there are very specific readings that you want me to peruse, I might need additional access codes.

****

James:

Will you soon be sending me the paper that you want me to edit?

Owmapow

****

Owmapow:

I thought I sent it over, already. Here it is, again.

The paper is about using virtual reality with zebrafish as a drug-free means of coping with pain. Note the mention of the lack of randomized controlled data to adjudicate this method's effectiveness. Good luck!

James

****

James:

I attached my Track Changes version of your paper's abstract. I want to be certain that the reading level is suitable for the audience(s) you have in mind and that I am using the same meaning for terms/phrases that you intended. I am a stickler for being thrifty with reasoning.

Further, I want to pay attention not only to overarching qualities of your rhetoric, but also to your work's mechanics. Please specify which style sheet I ought to follow, e.g., Chicago, APA, or other.

If I am on the right track, then I will proceed with the rest of your document. This work is a pleasure to edit. I am attaching two versions of your abstract to make sure that I am flying in the correct direction.

Owmapow

****

James:

Attached please find your paper, edited. Given that I made over forty comments on your paper and that I made literally dozens and dozens of edits, I think we can consider this version a "first pass." At your convenience, please address the questions listed in the comments.

Overall, you and your colleagues' ideas are well organized and are well explicated. Most scientists are not as adept at expressing themselves as is your research team. I look forward to joining you.

Owmapow

****

Dear Dr. Middleton:

It is bad enough that I dream about documentation when I am compiling the results of my own research. For the last few nights, I have been drifting to sleep thinking about my edits to your work and about corrections I would like to make to those edits. I'm glad I prefaced that I considered my most recent communication to you a "first pass."

I am eager to work with you on a more polished version of your article and to help finesse additional reports on your research. I was sincere when I expressed that I enjoy manipulating fascinating ideas. Your team's research certainly, and appropriately, commands attention.

I look forward to hearing from you.

Sincerely,
Owmapow

****

Dear Owmapow,

Thanks. I am in Cancun, now, at the International Ichthyology Conference and will, hopefully, get to check some of your work between meetings. If you have changes, please send them. Although I did not get to review your editing, I must tell you that the most important issue for me is hiring someone to write so I can use my time on other aspects of the project.

I am looking for a person who can read relevant material and do more than editing—maybe a person who can even refer to any relevant papers that we failed to cite. In brief, I must stop spending time on writing. So, please remember, in your editing and in your remarks, be very concise. Please!

Thanks,
James

****

Dear James:

I hope your conference was productive. I find such meetings are most valuable for the connections that they afford me, rather than for the opportunities that they provide for me to present or to listen to research; reliable studies find their way into print, anyway.

Speaking of print, I offered to provide you with a two-hour sample of my content. I certainly can, as well, search and read materials that are relevant to, but not yet included in, your manuscripts. However, doing so would require more than the two hours we negotiated.

More so, since I am an academic with my own research, I need to know whether or not you want to hire me. If so, we can discuss schedules/deadlines. If not, I've already given you much more than two hours of my time and can't afford to donate any more of it.

Sincerely,
Owmapow

****

Owmapow:

Agreed! Per conferences' value, though, I disagree. Conferences enable me to learn a lot about new developments before they get into print.

James

****

James:

I spent some time creating a document pertaining to hiring me.
I wrote out a job description, a salary chart, and so forth. Please
forgive me if any of this material is extraneous to your needs. I know
you are pressed for time. Accordingly, I thought it would be more
sagacious to send you lots of data than to volley limited data back
and forth.

I proposed a starting date of December 2nd as a compromise
between your need to get your science writer working "yesterday,"
and my need to "batten down the hatches" of my life. Please feel free
to communicate any questions, concerns, or corrections.

Sincerely,
Owmapow

****

Owmapow:

I did not read your paperwork carefully, but, per my glance, it looks
good.

James

****

James:

I am not familiar with the protocol for the Finley Institute of
Nature. Is there is a Human Resources Department that might have
procedures that I need to abide? Is there a confidentiality clause I
need to sign? Is there clearance that I must obtain? Other?

Once the paperwork is signed, I can immediately begin to read
current, related studies. Since I must put closure on others of my
projects, at present, I can't commit to anything more. Also, at the

juncture at which I am officially in your employ, I'll need passwords to those medical databases.

I hope that my paperwork can be completed in a timely fashion.

Sincerely,
Owmapow

****

James:

Hi! It seems that the next step for hiring me is for you to contact the Finley Institute of Nature Human Resources Dept.

Sincerely,
Dr. Owen Brownstone

****

Dear Dr. Middleton:

I last time that I heard from you was on Nov. 11. In brief, are you hiring me? If not, please advise, accordingly, so that I can take advantage of other opportunities.

Sincerely,
Dr. Owen Brownstone

Postscript: regardless, I would like to be reimbursed for the work I have already completed. In my email to you, of Oct. 11, I quoted you a price of $140.00. Although I worked in greater detail than required, and although I worked for a significantly longer period than two hours, I would like to receive, in the least, that figure and to receive it soon.

****

Dear Owmapow:

I got to talk with Human Resources and found out that the process for hiring a consultant is quite slow and requires paperwork (which I hate). I attached documents for you to fill out.

While we are waiting, I would like to hire you on another paper and would like to pay for it separately. As per the first paper, I did not receive a bill from you, yet. Please send one.

Thanks,
James

****

Dear James:

Per my prior free-lance work, I am charging you only $140.00, for two hours, the token amount of time for which I said I'd charge. My efforts took closer to twenty hours. The work required not just my response to the mechanics of the work, but also my response to the paper's content. In the future, I will have to charge more fully for my efforts.

As per the invoice, I am making progress. I do not like free-lance work as much as I like salaried work. As an academic, I am accustomed to letting someone else file my papers and to merely note when payments are deposited in my bank account.

No matter. Should we reach an employment agreement, I would require an hourly rate of $120.00/hour, for a minimum of ninety hours per month, for at least sixth months.

I would love to work for you. Your research is important to society as well as is fascinating to me!

Owmapow

****

Dear Owmapow:

I did not have the time to unearth all the details, but I believe hiring you as a consultant, rather than as staff, would save me money. Please let me know when you can come over for an interview and I can file the necessary forms.

James

****

James:

Sounds great! Please advise as to when I should arrive. Beyond my forms, do you need anything else?

Owmapow

****

Owmapow:

There's no need to bring anything else. Just try to complete the forms I sent you before your arrival so that I can submit them.

James

****

James:

Hi. I filled in my data. Your data (e.g., your signature, official job title, etc.) and Finery Institute of Nature's data will need to be filled in when I am on campus. Would next Monday, at 4:00 p.m., suit you for a meeting?

Owmapow

****

Owmapow:

Sounds good. Please call me to confirm the exact timing that morning.

James

****

Dear William:

How are you?

As per me, during the past few years, I've done a bit of teaching and a bit of non-academic writing. Now, I am on the cusp of being hired as a Senior Science Writer at the Finery Institute of Nature, an international science center, as a consultant for Dr. James Middleton, Department of Neurobiology, Faculty of Biology.

Dr. Middleton researches pain management. Dr. Middleton is smart, resourceful, and personable. FIN hired him as one of their Senior Scientists. That smart, nice guy is both well-funded and extremely busy. As such, he needs a science writer.

He expressed an interest in hiring me, but his HR Department wants the usual, requisite papers. Among those papers is a letter of recommendation. Dr. Middleton already has a sample of my work. At this point, what I need is one credible source to testify that I am a reliable worker, a critical and creative thinker, and a professional communicator.

My responsibilities will encompass conceptualizing, initiating, researching, writing, editing, and revising documents, publications, and other materials on pain management, as needed by Dr. Middleton and his staff. While in direct communication with Dr. Middleton's team, I will generate and review scientifically based materials for accuracy, and will develop peer-review journal articles, conference abstracts, presentations, internal background papers, clinical/statistical reports, and study protocols. I will also manage all subsequent journal/staff interaction, as well as will coordinate the submission of materials to conference panel organizers. Furthermore, I will "translate" the team's findings for both lay and technical audiences, into issue briefs, manuscripts, background papers, web materials and other documents, and will answer Finley Institute of Nature's staff's questions about the research findings of Dr. Middleton's group.

Would you mind writing a short letter of recommendation for me? I am supposed to bring that document with me when I next meet Dr. Middleton. However, if you are more comfortable emailing it directly to him, his email address is: J.Middleton@FIN.edu.

I appreciate your help with this matter.

Owmapow

PS: Meanwhile, I've been doing a bit of creative writing. Below are links to some of my recently published short works. I've been a bit stymied, though, getting my book-length manuscripts published.

****

Hello Owmapow,

I'm glad to hear that you are pressing ahead with so many activities. I'm including my letter in this email. Of course, Dr. Middleton will receive my email address, should he wish further communication.

Best!
William

Dec. 7, 2027
Dr. James Middleton
Department of Neurobiology
Faculty of Biology

Finley Institute of Nature

Dear Dr. Middleton:

I am pleased to serve as a reference for Dr. Owen Brownstone in his application for your position as a Senior Science Writer.

I first met Owen about 20 years ago when our paths often crossed at biology conferences, especially at those focused on oceanic studies. Owen struck me as being an insightful thinker. Additionally, he was energetic about putting together courses, programs, and research.

I participated in his program "Estuary Beauties," at the Oceanic Conference on International Studies in Moscow, and on his panel, "Is Water Pollution a Catalyst for Growth?" at the Ecology of Oceans Conference in Zürich. I found him to be thoughtful, efficient, and responsive in prodding participating scholars to execute and complete their speeches in a timely fashion. I should add that Owen, himself, put together a very innovative treatment of starfish ecology.

As is clear from his CV, Owen has maintained his teaching and professional connections over decades. I can attest that he continues to be very well regarded in the field not only as a teacher, but also in view of his original scholarship and his disciplinary leadership. His work is known for its ability to leverage theory and to throw light on practical biological problems.

Please contact me if I may be of further service as a reference.

Sincerely Yours,
J. William Novartis
Professor
Department of Environmental Science, Policy & Management
College of Natural Resources
University of California—Berkley

Berkeley, California 94720-5800
510-627-385
drjwnovartis@ucb.edu

****

Dear James:

Thank-you for making the time to meet with me. Your work is fascinating. I would love to be part of your team. I could begin work as soon as we sign a contract.

You mentioned a monthly rate. Please realize, as a free-lancer, I need to cover mileage and other expenses. Also, how many hours of work, per month, would this position entail?

Owmapow

****

Dear Owmapow:

The figure I quoted you was for the advertised four days per week, six to eight hours per day, job. I had hired another person for that position before you applied. I assume I ought to pay you similarly.

James

****

James:

I am a little bit confused. In my earlier email to you, I had stated the industry norm, per hour, for free-lancers who are experienced writers and editors. You had agreed to that rate. Nonetheless, you are offering me a wage far below that standard. I would like to work for you, but only if I work for a fair wage.

Owmapow

****

Owmapow:

I will process the paperwork as agreed. Until then, it will have to be as I wrote earlier. In other words, you will receive "pay per project." Accordingly, you will have to estimate the net number of hours any specific project will take and then you will have to let me know the total cost according to that rate. I am sure we will come to an agreement.

Best regards,
James

****

Owmapow:

I am awaiting FIN's HR Dept.'s reply regarding your first invoice. If they cannot accept it, I will find another way to pay you. In the worst case, I can pay you cash, but you will need to sign some forms to receive that money. In addition, it will not be easy for me to tell the scientific writer that I recruited before you showed up to "go home," so, you are stuck with piecemeal assignments.

James

****

James:

I finally filled out my consulting paperwork. I seem to be lacking FIN's tax number. Please convey it. Sorry for the long delay in sending you these papers.

Owmapow

****

Hi Owen:

I do not know FIN's tax #. Also, as far as I remember you did not yet send me a bill!!

James

****

James:

Please call the appropriate office on your campus and secure the tax number. As for the receipt, you did not like the informal one I issued to you. I cannot create a formal one without an institutional tax number.

Owen

****

Marty:

What is the FIN's tax number for consultants? When you answer me, please cc drowenbrownstone@SCU.edu?

Thanks,
James

****

Dr. Middleton:

I have yet to receive any money for the services I rendered to you over a year ago.

Dr. Owen Brownstone

****

Owen:

We are waiting for your bill before I make payments.

James

Owmapow's Side Job

Dr. Owen Brownstone:

I have organized a Science Writing course for a small group at my academy, but the intended instructor is suddenly unavailable. Would you be interested?

Please be in touch—the course is scheduled to start next week. My number is 766-4342. Alternatively, you could message me via Facebook.

Thank you.
Liad Filot

****

Liad:

It was nice to speak with you on the phone. I look forward to meeting with you on Monday morning, at 9:30. Meanwhile, I await my contract. I understand that I will begin work on Wednesday.

Attached, please find my CV. Per writing samples, please see the links, below, to "Crustaceans in Deep Space," in *Astral Flora and Fauna*, "The Care and Feeding of Rabid Hedgehogs" in *Smarmy Friends*, "The Elephant's Toe" in *Crazed Critters*, and "Squamata's Big Dance" in *Squeaks and Roars*.

After I've scanned, countersigned, and returned the contract to you,

I'll work on the syllabus. If there is anything more you need from me, please let me know. I look forward to joining your staff.

Owen

****

Owen:

Your contract is attached. It's informal but suffices.

Liad.

****

Dwayne:

Emailing me incomplete homework hours before a class meeting is NOT the way to succeed. You are falling significantly behind. When you miss class, you miss discussions of homework, and, more importantly, you miss all the class' vital syntheses of ideas. I will neither spend extra time responding to your work because you emailed it to me, in lieu of showing up to class, nor will I spend extra time catching you up on weeks' worth of classroom goings-on. I suggest that you show up next week, ON TIME, and that you show up to all subsequent class meetings.

Otherwise, consider dropping this course. There are other schools as well as private teachers that offer online lessons if you dislike face-to-face learning. Additionally, if your life is complicated by challenges, there are resources available for addressing them.

Frustratedly,
Dr. Owen Brownstone

****

Dr. Brownstone:

I emailed the homework as a practical substitute for printing it. I didn't expect you to follow up or to tutor me. Do not spend any extra time on my behalf! I know I'm falling behind, but it's my choice. I'm not expecting or asking for assistance. I'm giving your course my best effort… I'm taking part in it as much as I can. I know I'm not on the level of my classmates. Still, I know it's up to you to decide if I qualify for the certificate of mastery.

I'm gaining a lot from the course and am enjoying it. Perhaps, I'm not working at the highest level. Yet, I'm gaining enough that the course is worthwhile. If you feel my behavior bothers you or the other students, I will consider withdrawing. Until then, since I'm gaining from the course, I plan to continue. I will try my best to come on time, etc. Thanks for your concern.

Dwayne

****

Dwayne:

Students must print their homework and bring it with them to class. It is my job, as your instructor, to help where needed. My help, though, can't substitute for your homework or for your attendance.

You are an intelligent young man possessed of wonderful rudimentary skills. Classes are for developing what's already innate. Please come to class.

"Certificate?" Whereas you are lacking in both attendance and homework, you cannot pass the class let alone receive any notice of merit.

Dr. Brownstone

****

Owen:

Please do not address students so forcefully. Also, PLEASE do not suggest that they need help in life; it is very insulting.

I thought we agreed that I would speak with Dwayne. I will do so softly, but firmly. He is in my History of The United States course. He shows up for it, so don't tell me or him that he's not showing up for classes at all.

Liad

****

Liad:

Oh! I took for granted certain things, such as the integrity of this program. Related, what is meant by students "receiving a certificate of mastery" at the completion of this course? Had Dwayne not mention such a document, I would not have known about it. Please fill me in on the specifics.

Owen (Owmapow)

****

Owmapow:

Sorry, the sent button got pressed by accident. What I meant to say was "Phew! What a relief! We are lucky that Dwayne is a generous person. It could very well have gone the other direction. I don't like legal dealings. Even without litigious communications, we must protect the reputation of our school.

Going forward, please, please, even though you may be right, tread cautiously when interacting with students. Thank-you very much.

Don't worry about the certificate. It's an administrative matter. I'll take care of sending them out.

Liad Filot

****

Dr. Brownstone:

Hi. It's Dwayne Gilunk from your Science Writing course. Sorry to disturb you. I'm working on next week's homework and I'm having a problem. I tried opening the URLs for the second and third readings, but the URLs didn't work. I then tried the key words and they, too, didn't work. I would appreciate some helps. Thanks!

Dwayne

****

Dwayne:

It could be your browser. I have been having trouble with Firefox this past week and, hence, switched to Chrome. I just checked the homework's URLs via Chrome and both URLs worked.

Dr. Brownstone

****

Hi Liad!

The course has been completed. I stayed after class to evaluate the exams before handing them in, graded, to your administrative assistant. I met each class for three full academic hours, prepared lectures and homework, provided office hours, evaluated students' work, and otherwise completed the tasks with which I had been charged. Now, I need to be paid. Simply, you owe me $4,000.

Owen Brownstone

****

Owen:

Thank you very much. Would you please send me the results of the evaluations so I can give your students their grades?

Liad

****

Liad:

Perhaps you overlooked the grades that I handed to your assistant. Each student's course grade is written and circled on the first page of their final. The other grade is their final's score. I've already noted as much in an email to you.

When will I receive the salary due to me?

Owen

****

Dr. Brownstone:

Hi! It's Harvey Salem, Liad's bookkeeper. If you did not yet do so, please send in your hours for the term. Please CC Liad. Nobody can get paid until their hours are in.

Thank you.

Harvey Salem

****

Dr. Brownstone:

I forwarded your email to Liad. I will let you know about the payment and about your receipt.

Harvey Salem

****

Harvey Salem:

Four months have passed since the end of the term, and I have not yet been paid.

Dr. Owen Brownstone

****

Liad Filot:

No, you cannot hold my salary hostage because you do not like the grades that I issued.

However, since I'm due to become a visiting scholar on the other side of the country in a matter of weeks, I did abide by your request to improve Dwayne Gilunk's grade from a "D" to a "C." Note that I also elevated all the other enrollees' grades by the same amount.

Please send me my salary. I recall that you don't like litigious actions.

Sincerely,
Dr. Owen Brownstone

Owmapow and the Unsolicited Request

Dr. Own Brownstone:

I've read some of your short stories. I'd like to invite you to join my team for an exciting project.

Dr. Vincent Bianchi

****

Dr. Bianchi:

What type of project are you facilitating?

Dr. Owen Brownstone

****

Dr. Brownstone:

I'll tell you all about it when we talk. Give me some time slots.

Dr. Bianchi:

****

Dr. Bianchi:

Let's try some time during between 11am and 5pm, Thursday. Would that work? Otherwise, I'm not available until next week.

Dr. Brownstone

****

Dr. Brownstone:

Noon, Thursday, suits me. My Skype id is: Bianchi@gmail.com

Dr. Bianchi

****

Dr. Bianchi:

It was nice speaking with you. I believe that I could contribute meaningfully to your project on oceanic narrative. I like writing littoral stories.

Here's a summary of the points I raised during our conversation:

* Joseph Campbell mentioned, in his great work, *The Masks of G-d*, that all narratives are variations of a single great story.

* It would be helpful to hire professionals from that New Jersey-based digital entertainment company to supply images.

* Flash fiction tales use up very little audio time. For example, a short story of mine, which was over three thousand words long, took only seven minutes in audio form. A flash would take far less time.

* Narrative has a multitude of applications. Consider the YouTube video that I posted that compares the mating habits of walpurtis with those of weedy sea dragons. https://www.youtube.com/oceanicspecies/mating/=seadragonsorwalpurtis.

* Narrative is most effective when written for an audience. For whom am I making the templates? Investors? Screeners? Other? Are those persons wise about the ways of sea life? It would help me to

know as much as possible about your intended audience.

*Format: maybe a dropdown box, or a similar interface with a hierarchy of topics, would be constructive. For instance, under "fish," you could put the subtopics: "hagfish," "lampreys," "cartilaginous," "ray-finned bony," and "lobe-finned bony." In turn, each of those subtopics could branch to sub-subtopics. More choices could create addional consumer interest.

* I'd like a combination of a fixed fee contract and stock. On balance, "nothing is anything until it is something." That is, I am willing to partition my remuneration for only a limited period. While you're empire building, I'm still paying bills. I'm willing to take time from others of my projects only if I can receive some upfront monies from you.

Dr. Owen Brownstone
(Owmapow)

PS: After your company goes public, thousands of scripts will be needed for folks who become "addicted" to your channel, i.e., for people who become addicted to tinkering with wildlife narratives. Additional writers will have to be hired. I know many writers who would be good hires. Let me know when you are ready for their contact information.

****

Owmapow:

I got your email. Currently, I'm bombarded with sales targets, delivery issues, and prepping for my trip to Russia. I can't get into deep discussions.

I agree with you about advertising and demographics. However, our fish tales need to be mainstream. For now, I need to focus on broad-based entertainment.

You requested a mix of remuneration. That's tough since I don't have the time to figure out a conversion from sweat equity to actual money. As soon as the prototype brings in funding, I can send cash.

How long would it take for you to develop a few short-short stories as well as to develop a list of key words to use for blanks in those stories? What's your fee?

Vinnie

****

Vinnie:

I grok brief emails and am okay with gaps between volleys. In fact, I'm entirely logged off most weekends. Please send me a more detailed set of specs for those short-shorts. What's more, should I aim for texts that read for about a minute?

Orro (an Australian expression of closure used by an editor whom I adore),

Owmapow

****

Vinnie:

Attached, please find two scripts. Please advise if they are what you are seeking.

Given introductory and closing music of approximately three to five seconds, apiece, the stories, themselves, will fill fifty seconds or less of airtime. Please do not use soundtracks like those featured on *Jaws*. Most aquatic encounters are far less dramatic.

Nighty-Night,
Owmapow

****

Owmapow:

Thank you for your samples. I'm not sure that either of them suits me. The texts are a bit long, and they lack a list of fillers. Also, they need to be simpler and funnier. Their reading level is way too high. I understand your challenge.

Also, for now, I want our prototype to focus on newscasts. See http://vimeo.com/67832415 for an example. That story about piranhas typifies what I am seeking.

Vinnie

****

Vinnie:

The broadcast was helpful. I better grasp your intended audience's reading level and the role of sounds and images in your project.

To wit, attached, please find some new stories. The blank spaces among lines are meant to be filled in with music and pictures. These new stories are sufficiently vague as to be enjoyable to a wide array of people. Please let me know if I am approaching your concept.

Owmapow

****

Owmapow:

My initial reaction is that your work's still a bit "out there." I'll get back to you.

Vinnie

****

Owmapow:

I soaked in your tales for a while. I'm confounded. Your writing is too stylized. Your language is too good. For my needs, plots and diction must be more down to earth. I think you are still not understanding what I am seeking.

Our users must be able to relate to our narratives. Think species' evolution. Think global warming or other climate change factors. Our consumers need to be able to drag/drop down events into your stories, and then to reshape them as their own. "Their" stories will include bits from Internet science sites, environmental broadcasts, and so on.

For starters, we need just a few plots, such as: fish meets fish, fish eats fish, or fishes spawn. The length of your examples is right, but your tales of tails (ha ha) still lack wide appeal. Later, maybe, can we aim for more particular audiences. For our prototype, we require mainstream work.

Vinnie

****

Vinnie:

When I write up the next versions, I will ask some of my college students to read them. I think they belong to the demographic that you're targeting.

Owmapow

****

Owmapow:

No hurry. I am off the grid for a bit.

Vinnie

****

Vinnie:

The co-eds say I should simplify my stories' plots, that is, that I ought to make my samples more linguistically frugal. No matter, Version Three is attached. Please let me know if it's closer to what you are seeking. I dropped the complex language while retaining the narratives' freshness.

Owmapow

****

Owmapow:

I had to take time to really get through this version, which is odd considering that the stories are brief. More specifically, any stories we use must be more grounded. So, no more pink sea cucumbers or frilled sharks, please. Also, while I like your whimsical approach, that style doesn't help our engineers transform stories into my prototype. Please write more plainly. Furthermore, your tales shouldn't focus on marine geology or on chemical oceanography. Those topics are too highbrow for our initial audience. Have a look at the newscasts, again.

Vinnie

****

Vinnie:

Version Four is attached. I let my student "consultants" test-drive this version. It worked for them as being sufficiently interesting and flexible (albeit a handful of emerging adults is an infinitely small sample of the millions of available social media users.)

Owmapow

****

Owmapow:

This newest version is on the right track. Moving forward, I need your scripts to tie into events like those taking place between hatching and mating or between fighting off a predator and mating. You get the idea. Also, I need more blanks in each story so that we can add lots of music and images.

While you are rewriting, I will work with my software crew to provide Internet inserts. Next, we'll merge your stories with those data.

Vinnie

****

Vinnie:

I'm back at the keyboard. Attached is a "rethink." It contains six, not two, tales. Please let me know if I am getting closer to your vision.

Owmapow

****

Vinnie:

Any word?

Owmapow

****

Owmapow:

Your scripts are nowhere close to what I need. I don't think you will be part of the team, going forward. Thanks for your contributions.

Vinnie

Owmapow the Incorrigible

Dear Freelance Science Editors:

I am not sending this email bcc since you will be meeting each other at the seminar. Please confirm your participation to scied@CIT.edu. Use "Attention: Science Editors' Workshop" as your subject. If you require a parking permit, please also submit your car's registration number, make, and color, and your mobile phone number. Even if you need no permit, please attach your CV to your response.

You will join our freelance editors' team and will aid our scholars with their research proposals for the National Science Institute.

The topic deadlines are:

Nov. 05: Medicine, and Social Sciences

Nov. 13: Atmospheric and Earth Sciences, Chemistry, Computer Sciences, Ecology, Systematic Biology, Oceanography, and Physics

Let me know if you have topic preferences or questions. I look forward to meeting and working with you.

Best Regards,
Shai-Li Vallo
Head

Scientific Publications Department
California Institute of Technology

****

Ms. Vallo:

Finally! My papers are attached. Please let me now if anything
is missing. My references are from CEOs of small presses—they
produced my *Crustaceans Never End*, and my *Hedgehogs and Lobsters*,
respectively. Also, you've not yet told me how many hours per week
are required for each project. Please advise.

Dr. Owen Brownstone

****

Hi Owen Brownstone:

Attached are the forms that will clarify what is required from our
freelance editors.

Best,
Shai-Li Vallo

****

Hello All,

My name is Yasmin Poola and I'll be attending the CIT editing
workshop. I'd be happy to share expenses with anyone willing to
drive. I live in Los Feliz. Please contact me immediately.

Thanks,
Yasmin

****

Hi Owen,

I just spoke to Gaya. She lives in Burbank and is willing to take us in her car if we can get to the Burbank Sonoco station. She said she'd leave around 9:15. She's going to speak with Liel Alves about picking her up, also.

I think, after all, I'll take the bus. There's one leaving at 8:30 that gets to Pasadena at a little after 10:00, thus giving me time to find the meeting place and then to have some coffee. There's another bus leaving at 9:15 that arrives at Pasadena at 10:51. Let me know if you want to ride the bus with me.

Yasmin

****

Yasmin:

I think I'll go with Gaya since I live close to Burbank. Worse case, I will drive myself to the seminar. Have you worked for CIT in the past?

Owen

****

Dear Owen Brownstone:

Thanks for forms. I tried to "send" them into the system, but it appears that one of the forms must be signed by your accountant or bank manager.

Best,
Shai-Li Vallo

****

Ms. Vallo:

Scans of my forms, including the one that had to be signed by my bank manager, are attached. Do you need anything more before our meeting? What is the agenda? What volume of work do you anticipate? What is the compensation? I must raise funds for the care and feeding of a new tank of Pacific Lamprey.

Owen Brownstone

****

Good Morning Shai-Li!

It was lovely to meet you, Mila, and Emily. I am wowed by your organizational skills; it takes a great command of resources to funnel so many sets of data through such a short time frame.

As per me, I'm happy to report that in terms of form and content, the government documents, which your employees finesse, are similar to the papers I've produced as a professor (I'm an oceanographer by training.) Hence, I'm that much more than eager to accept your assignments. Are your remuneration rates closer to 150 or to 200 dollars per hour?

Warmly,
Owmapow (Owen Brownstone)

****

Yasmin:

Hi! Have you heard from CIT, yet? I've heard nothing.

Owmapow

****

Owmapow:

I haven't heard a thing. I'm glad, though, since I have something else to finish before undertaking any new work.

Yasmin

****

Dear Brona Marshe,

Our Scientific Publications Department will provide editing services for NIS proposals submitted by your new hires, including those starting at CIT during this year's fall semester. Your faculty should send their proposals directly to me. Be aware that tenured faculty, too, will be requiring our services.

To wit, attached, please find a list of our freelance editors and of their areas of specialization. Your people are welcome to contact them directly if that arrangement better suits them.

Best Regards,
Shai-Li Vallo
Head
Scientific Publications Department

****

Good Morning Shai-Li!

When will we new editors receive assignments?

Owmapow

****

Dear Owmapow:

The work is only dribbling in, so, for now, we are using only in-house editors.

Shai-Li

****

Dear Owmapow:

Can you handle this one? Let me know. Use Track Changes and then return the material to me.

Best,
Shai-Li

****

Dear Shai-Li:

Absolutely!

Owmapow

****

Hi Owmapow:

I will be reviewing your edits but won't be able to get to them before next Thursday, so Wednesday is your deadline. Per remuneration, the official rate of seventy dollars per double spaced page is what we're offering unless I find that a particular proposal requires major effort (I don't believe that any recent proposals require "major effort.")

Best,
Shai-Li

****

Hi Shai-Li!

I'm hoping to get most of this piece worked on during this weekend's remaining hours. When you count pages, are you counting submitted pages or edited pages? The former will almost always be more than the latter.

Owmapow

****

Hi Shai-Li!

Gee whiz! There's a ton of fluff in this research proposal. Attached is my Track Changes version of just its abstract. Ought I to proceed with editing or wait until the primary investigator receives these edits?

Owmapow

****

Dear Owmapow

While the abstract needed smoothing out and supplementation, you overedited. Your role is to make the text fluid, not to rewrite it. Also, you were tasked to point out where there is missing information and to make suggestions about how to fill in those gaps, not to actually fill them in.

Finally, it was unnecessary for you to edit the proposal's references for consistency. All that you ought to have done was to check whether documentation was used in a coherent manner. I highlighted these points in the attached file.

Best,
Shai-Li

****

Shai-Li:

Is it possible to contact you tonight? I would like to continue to edit my assigned proposal, but I don't want to invest any more time in it before I am entirely sure that I can fully follow the parameters of this job. Once I "get the gist" of your system, I will be able to move rapidly through my work. A brief phone call could help, too. Taking everything into account, I'm glad I erred on the side of "too much" rather than of "too little" refinement.

Owmapow

****

Dear Shai-Li Vallo:

I am a Ph.D. who was once a National Science Foundation Scholar (Eastern New Mexico University's Biology Department). I had my first academic paper published within a year of my completing my terminal degree. I was *invited* to respond, orally, and in writing, to many national conference programs, too. Further, I was an invited guest editor for *Ocean and Coastal Management*. What's more, fairly recently, I helped some internationally known postdocs reshape a chapter, which was subsequently accepted for a state-of-the-art book. Also, I regularly teach science writing and editing.

Whereas I am sure that you receive much balderdash from pompous academics with underdeveloped social skills, their sounding off doesn't excuse poor writing. Plus, whereas I know you're counting down to retirement, it remains the case that we, your editors, deserve even-handedness when given assignments.

Said differently, I am a critical thinker who has spent his entire life helping others achieve linguistic parsimony. In short, something that snorts, has a mane, and has a long tail might be a zebra or a giraffe, but is most likely a horse. Similarly, *Geotria australis* is not identical to *Entosphenus tridentatus* and never will be. Poor writing cannot be gussied up to become sound writing except to an audience consisting of dupes or their kin.

I spent hours in government offices and at the bank completing the forms you sent me. I spent time at your editors' seminar. I used parts of several days to assess the abstract you emailed to me.

Even so, I must decline engaging in any additional work for CIT. While I need the income to feed my eels, and while I enjoy highlighting the nuances of others' ideas, I also need to trust that my decades of science writing and science editing experience remain valid. Accordingly, please assign the proposal that you sent to me to someone else.

I hope you will compensate me for my time.

Sincerely,
Dr. Owen Brownstone

Owmapow's Sister

Hi Owen!

Even though we don't talk much, you're my only sibling. Excepting your lowbrow humor, expressed in your annual birthday salutation; "Greetings to Dr. Brownstone at Brown (University of) Stone," I rarely hear from you. So, I'm asking you to look over some of my newest ideas. Note: I'm seeking funding from The Association of Senior University Women.

My ideas follow;

Our society is composed of many types of people but is guided by only a fraction of them. There exists a dearth of information on communication ethics, in general, and on the ethics of communicating voter options, more explicitly. Often, persons charged with social responsibility seem unable to extricate themselves from the quag created by the rhetoric/philosophy nexus. To boot, policy makers, time and again, muddle descriptions about their ethical accountability to the nation and to its citizens. Mysteries abound around the hegemonical factors coloring the election process. We need to: transcend the usual gamut of voter experiences, allow political discussions to become more generally accessible, and show how communication morality is an applied process.

We must contextualize formal treatments of topics as limited by human understanding of occurrences' contexts and by human articulations therefrom. Consider recent race riots and consider pandemic-influenced business losses. Our limitations in grasping *a priori* propositions, when negotiating the importance and expression of goings-on's, cause us to simultaneously, and confusingly, legitimize conflicting views.

To address these concerns, my study will test statements about morality's implicit and explicit impressions on the discourse of public parties and on the discourse about consciousness raising in citizens', politicians', and institutions' communication. This research will inspect links among communication ethics, invention, identity, and ideology as those links apply to interpersonal, group, and mass media impediments. It will provide, as well, details about creativity, designation, and theory building's morally significant interactions. Additionally, this study will probe ways in which the muddling of individual and institutional roles impact public policy and freedom.

For data, this study will gauge federal government, national newscast, and private individual's election communications and will assess metacommunications of the same. It will utilize at least five hundred samples and will lay emphasis on alleged:

> shared accountability among institutions, politicians, and citizens to each other
>
> joint accountability to citizens by institutions and politicians
>
> joint accountability to politicians by institutions and citizens
>
> joint accountability to institutions by citizens and politicians
>
> accountability to citizens by institutions
>
> accountability to citizens by politicians
>
> accountability to institutions by politicians
>
> accountability to institutions by citizens
>
> accountability to politicians by citizens
>
> accountability to politicians by institutions

Philosophical *topoi* illuminating language's pre-established messages tend to ignore language's processes. Such communications tend to discount information about texts and events since they pose social narrative primarily as imperative discourse. What's more, context-free quantitative linguistic analysis is problematic for resolving that complexity as such analysis tends to discard data generated by communication's progressions and as such analysis fails to show the range of dialectical phenomena, establish norms for those phenomena, and describe human influences on those phenomena.

Therefore, this study's findings will be interpreted via rhetorical criticism. More exactly, its data will be filtered to reveal their normative dimension, i.e., undergirding moral philosophy; descriptive dimension, i.e., cultural morality; and metatheoretical dimension, i.e., metatheories of morality.

Last, in its evaluation phase, this study will: link constructs among ideologies, icons, and virtue, make palpable the influence of individually and socially held beliefs about communication morality on communication about elections, and contrast contemporary means of resolving mercurial moral systems. Further, it will measure coercion, consensus, compromise, and systems of ranking (including hierarchy and prayer), and will calculate how the results of these schemes, respectively, create understanding, conviction, and emotional stases of comparative worth.

I hope that this study will demonstrate the link between invention and communication morality, too. It will explicate: the connection between conceptual genesis and conceptual differentiation, some corollaries of creativity on communication uniformity, and some effects of sound bites, units of consequence, and forms of media on the transferability of ideas.

Communication ethics are best informed by the utilitarian similitude between meaning and morality. Techniques that illuminate the intersection of deeds and words and that incorporate the best of experientialism and of objectivism empower us. Weigh that balloting is psychological, not logical. In view of that truth, this study is needed.

Owen, thanks, in advance, for your input.

Love,
Rachel

****

Sis:

I am sorry that it has taken me so long to get back to you. After my female butterfly ray birthed seven pups, three of my males were fighting to reimpregnate her. I had to place her and her litter in a second aquarium to protect them from the males' aggressions.

Anyway, I'm here, now. Attached, please find some of my work on communication ethics. I envision my essays as book chapters. I have long sought to co-author a project with you. I'm open to reasonable presentations/representations/modifications of my work.

As you know, I'm fond of writing books. Do you ever think about the years that I spent fashioning *Estuary Creature Delights* and *Deep Water Creature Delights*? I believe that my ideas, in conjunction with yours, will find funding and will quickly receive a book contract. I'm willing to work to solicit peer critiques of our project.

Please recall, too, that early on, while midwifing ocean critters, I forever talked about the nature of "good," and of "bad." Additionally, before that period, I had articulated a strong response to Mom's militancy about chores and allowance.

My attachments on communication ethics are worthy of your time. I'm glad that you shared some of your newest ideas with me.

Love,

Owmapow

****

Dear Big Brother:

When we were small, you included me in four square games and
taught me how to pitch a softball. Moreover, you encouraged my
scholarship from kindergarten, onward. If not for you, I might not
have known the difference between a rhombus and a parallelogram,
or between a pyramid and a tetrahedron, at least until I learned how
to read.

While you are a great brother, a kind man, an insightful instructor,
and an enviable lover of wildlife, we have located ourselves in
distinctly different academic fields. In addition, you and I dwell at
different levels of the scholarly strata.

In short, sibling dear, I cannot risk my reputation by having a family
member, who works outside of my discipline, co-author my research.
In fact, my forthcoming study is so important that I'll invite only a
dozen or so of my most perceptive graduate students to complete the
attendant grunt work.

I asked for your feedback because the politicizing of academia
has made me reluctant to talk to my peers about these ideas.
The existence of powers that have turned the ivory tower into an
ideological bayou have reinforced the need for my study. Yet, it's
essential that my ideas get presented in a peer-reviewed journal or,
better, as a book by a scholarly press! When I attain those ambitions,
my thoughts might, with luck, incite a handful of respected thinkers
to raise questions about the pedagogical status quo.

Unfortunately, academic governance looks unfavorably on folks
lacking my credentials. More to the point, as my lone sibling, and as
a man with a broad, albeit empirical, focus (my work remains reliant
on hermeneutics), I feel safe asking for your regard, but not for your

content.

Whereas rhetoricians and philosophers have long dealt with the topic of communication ethics, biologists have not. My research concentrates on words' meanings in relationship to actions' magnitudes.

You study the causality of ecosystems. Yes, you've had success teaching science writing, a species of applied rhetoric. Nonetheless, I hold you as better at describing cartilaginous and lobe-finned fish than at describing enthymemes and *ethos*.

My emphasis on how communication ethics shapes creativity, self-concept, and modes of transmitting beliefs is very unlike your focus on shelled beings. I know nothing of estuaries.

You know nothing of interpersonal persuasion, except as intention determines which of your male rays will mate with your females. Creature communication is not human communication.

Likewise, my knowledge of the last twenty-five hundred years of western ethics fails to overlap with your knowledge of saltwater diversity. Furthermore, where I want to espouse solutions to electoral college dilemmas, you're driven by pollution's bearings on *Cambarus aculabrum* and on overfishing's harm to *Orconectes*.

I appreciate your interest in my work. I'm thrilled that you support me. However, given that you lack the knowledge relevant to my endeavour, I cannot accept you as my co-author.

Love,
Sis

****

Dear Rachel:

I am deeply hurt by your assumption that I lack professional

proficiency researching ethics. For decades, my scholarship has
been dedicated to moral questions about interspecies interactions.
Besides, I have long attempted to create links between my research
and "commonplace" problems like the global water supply and
like the unenforced fishing limits of international waters. On other
occasions, you've admitted my focus as being such.

I want to enlighten the world about the ways in which our moral
attachments, or, unfortunately, our lack thereof, to shelled and
fleshy sea creatures have influenced our thinking. Toward that end,
I created an abridged history of the study of language as it is used in
oceanographic research. I, too, have published discussions concerning
ways in which academics ought to use their expertise to negotiate
widespread problems. Water pollution, coral reef death, and overfishing
affect us all.

I feel misunderstood. I also feel unfavorably and unnecessarily
judged.

Love,
Your Brother

****

Dear Owen:

For decades, I hated being your younger sister. I was always held
up to whatever you had accomplished. Although it was me who:
thought to add Ramshorns to your tank, raised goldfish fry for
profit (so that you could buy those extra exotics), and protested
our school's frog dissection requirement, you were the one that our
district lauded with awards. It was you, not me, who regularly had
his picture in the local paper.

Unsurprisingly, as a grownup, I turned my back on science. In its
place, I became betrothed to the humanities. At the same time as
I never doubted your genius or your sensitivity, for the sake of my

sanity, I had to distance myself from you. Like your beaten male stingrays, I "fail" when rivaled.

I have never intended to become your appendage. I am a middle-aged woman with unique feelings, who is an adept in her own right.

It behooves you to think of me as an intellectual with exceptional merits rather than as your kid sister. If I look to you, it's not to invite you to improve my work, but to ask you to validate it. I allowed myself to become vulnerable by sending you my research ideas as an (apparently lame) attempt to better our connection. I would never ask your permission, per se, for my scholarship. Owen, you can do better!

Love,
Sis

****

Rachel:

I always thought that Mom and Dad loved you best. I can't believe you've long resented me. I was always jealous of you. You were the smarter, more attractive, and more popular child.

Your activities were touted to relatives. Mine were minimalized. Remember my full college scholarship? Mom and Dad didn't applaud that achievement. More accurately, they asked me why I didn't also receive a housing stipend.

When I became an Assistant Professor, they asked me why I didn't start my career as an Associate Professor. When I received National Science Foundation monies, they told me that my award size was "embarrassingly small."

Inversely, when two boys asked you to the prom, that became our family's most newsworthy event for a full season. When you were offered early admission to an Ivy League school, our parents called all our aunts and uncles to crow about your success. When you received tenure, since Mom and Dad had just gotten Internet access, they posted your promotion on all their social media accounts.

I never tried to compete with you. Our parents' need to liken us to each other came from their own insecurities. I just wanted to be the best sibling I could be for you. I guess I mistakenly interpreted your email as an invitation to work together.

My departmental responsibilities, my summer job as a science writing instructor, and my volunteer hours as the manager of docents at a local science museum more than fill my schedule. As well, I became an active participant in the Association of Zoos and Aquariums' breeding program. I'm a busy guy.

Correspondingly, I don't need any more publications. Like you, I received tenure. I just wanted to relate to you.

I guess co-authoring is not the best way to be your sibling. How 'bout, instead, when you next present findings at any California-based conference, you join me for tacos? I'll order spicy for you and mild for me.

Love,
Owen

PS: Thanks for rescuing my fish and frogs from the pond after Dad made me throw them away and for giving them to Frank's brother to protect. I guess, like you, that brute proved to be okay.

Credits

"Around Once More with Owmapow." *Bewildering Stories*. May 2020.

"Beloved Little Sister." *Bewildering Stories*. Aug. 2021.

"Deep Sea Mothers." *Bewildering Stories*. Nov. 2015. Rpt. In *Friends and Rabid Hedgehogs*. Bards & Sages Publishing. Jun. 2016 and Rpt. in *Concatenation*. Omnibus. Bards & Sages Publishing. 2018.

"Dogged Dr. Brownstone" as "Dogged Dr. Owen." *Bewildering Stories*. Aug. 2019. Rpt. in *Demurral: Linens and Towels and Fears*. Bards & Sages Publishing. 2020.

"Fame and Fortune." *Bewildering Stories*. Sep. 2017. Rpt. in *Walnut Street*. Bards & Sages Publishing. 2019.

"Of Crustaceans and an Emerging Creative Writer." *Bewildering Stories*. Nov. 2015. Rpt. in *Friends and Rabid Hedgehogs*. Bards & Sages Publishing. Jun. 2016 and in *Concatenation*. Omnibus. Bards & Sages Publishing. 2018.

"Owmapow and the Unsolicited Request." *Spark!* Sep. 2020.

"Owmapow Gets Fired." *Bewildering Stories*. Nov. 2015. Rpt. in *Friends and Rabid Hedgehogs*. Bards & Sages Publishing. Jun. 2016 and in *Concatenation*. Omnibus. Bards & Sages Publishing. 2018.

"Owmapow Keeps Trying." *Bewildering Stories*. Mar. 2019. Rpt. in *Demurral: Linens and Towels and Fears*. Bards & Sages Publishing. 2020.

"Owmapow Rides Again." *Bewildering Stories*. May 2019. Rpt. in *Demurral: Linens and Towels and Fears*. Bards & Sages Publishing. 2020.

"Owmapow's Side Job." *Bewildering Stories*. Aug. 2020.

"Owmapow's Sister." *Bewildering Stories*. Feb. 2021.

"Owmapow the Incorrigible." *Bewildering Stories*. Nov. 2020.

"Shredded Paper." *Bewildering Stories*. Oct. 2016. Rpt. in *Can I be Rare, Too?* Bards & Sages Publishing. 2017 and in *Concatenation*. Omnibus. Bards & Sages Publishing. 2018.

Acknowledgments

Computer Cowboy and Younger Dude (Missy Older, Older Dude, and Missy Younger have since fledged) have been making do with tuna salad and folding their own laundry so that I could work on this manuscript. Thanks, guys!

As well, I'm grateful to Don Webb, Erika Cleveland, and Julie Ann Dawson for their roles in creating this book. Writers get into difficulties without support. Owmapow would have had more success if he had enjoyed similar backing.

About the Author

As KJ Hannah Greenberg sprouts more white hairs and grandchildren, she is increasingly focusing on fulfilling book contracts. She writes about: Judaism, parenting, imaginary hedgehogs, and starfaring, polycephalic, gelatinous wildebeests.

Earlier in life, Hannah played oboe, participated in martial arts, learned basket weaving, and studied Middle Eastern dancing. What's more, she became a certified herbalist, and an AP College Board-authorized calculus teacher. As a rhetoric professor, she mostly taught critical and creative thinking by means of English, communications, philosophy, sociology, and psychology courses and graciously accepted National Endowment for the Humanities funding.

As a creative writer, Hannah was nominated once for The Best of the Net in poetry, three times for the Pushcart Prize in Literature for poetry, once for the Pushcart Prize in Literature for fiction, once for the Million Writers Award for fiction, and once for the PEN/Diamonstein-Spielvogel Award for the Art of the Essay.

KJ Hannah Greenberg's Other Books

Fiction Collections

Demurral: Linens and Towels and Fears (Bards & Sages Publishing, 2020).

Walnut Street (Bards & Sages Publishing, 2019).

The omnibus, Concatenation (Bards & Sages Publishing, 2018).

Can I be Rare, Too? (Bards & Sages Publishing, 2017).

Friends and Rabid Hedgehogs (Bards & Sages Publishing, 2016).

Cryptids (Bards & Sages Publishing, 2015).

The Immediacy of Emotional Kerfuffles, 2nd ed. (Bards and Sages Publishing, 2015).

Don't Pet the Sweaty Things, 2nd ed. (Bards and Sages Publishing, 2014).

Novels and Musical

The Ill-Advised Adventures of Jim-Jam O'Neily (serialized in Bewildering Stories, 2022, Forthcoming).

Upon the Lion and the Serpent (Eden Stories Press, 2022, Forthcoming).

Ten Kilo and One Million (Crooked Cat Books, 2017).

My Neighbor Judy (serialized in Tachlis Magazine, 2017-2018).

Watercolors (Scotch & Soda Productions, 1979).

Essay Collections

Sweet and Sour: Womanly Thoughts (Seashell Books, 2021).

Simple Gratitudes (Propertius Press, 2020).

The omnibus, Smiling and Nodding with Alacrity (Seashell Books. 2020).

The Nexus of the Sun, the Moon, and Mother (Seashell Books, 2020).

Whistling for Salvation (Seashell Books, 2019).

On Golden Limestone (Seashell Books, 2018).

Rhetorical Candy (Seashell Books, 2018).

Tosh: Select Trash and Bosh of Creative Writing (Crooked Cat Books, 2017).

Dreams are for Coloring Books: Midlife Marvels (Seashell Books, 2017).

Word Citizen: Uncommon Thoughts on Writing, Motherhood & Life in Jerusalem (Tailwinds Press, 2015).

Jerusalem Sunrise: Veracious Celebrations (Imago Press, 2015).

Oblivious to the Obvious: Wishfully Mindful Parenting (French Creek Press, 2010).

Conversations on Communication Ethics (Praeger, 1991).

Poetry Collections

One-Handed Pianist (Hekate Publishing, 2021).

Flames and Fire (Seashell Books, 2021).

Rudiments (Seashell Books, 2020).

The Wife/Mom (Seashell Books, 2019).

Beast There—Don't That (Fomite Press, 2019).

Mothers Ought to Utter Only Niceties (UnboundCONTENT, 2017).

A Grand Sociology Lesson (Lit Fest Press, 2016).

Dancing with Hedgehogs (Fowlpox Press, 2014).

The Little Temple of My Sleeping Bag (Dancing Girl Press, 2014).

Citrus-Inspired Ceramics (Aldrich Press, 2013).

Intelligence's Vast Bonfires (Lazarus Media, 2012).

Supernal Factors (The Camel Saloon Books on Blog, 2012).

Fluid & Crystallized (Fowlpox Press, 2012).

A Bank Robber's Bad Luck with His Ex-Girlfriend (UnboundCONTENT, 2011).

Writing a review on social media sites for readers will help the progress of independent publishing. To submit a review, go to the book page on any of the sites and follow the links for reviews. Books from independent presses rely on reader-to-reader communications.

For more information or to order any of our books, visit:
http://www.fomitepress.com/our-books.html

More story collections from Fomite...

MaryEllen Beveridge — After the Hunger
MaryEllen Beveridge — Permeable Boundaries
Jay Boyer — Flight
L. M Brown — Treading the Uneven Road
L. M Brown — Were We Awake
Michael Cocchiarale — Here Is Ware
Michael Cocchiarale — Still Time
Neil Connelly — In the Wake of Our Vows
Catherine Zobal Dent — Unfinished Stories of Girls
Zdravka Evtimova — Carts and Other Stories
John Michael Flynn — Off to the Next Wherever
Derek Furr — Semitones
Derek Furr — Suite for Three Voices
Elizabeth Genovise — Where There Are Two or More
Andrei Guriuanu — Body of Work
Zeke Jarvis — In A Family Way
Arya Jenkins — Blue Songs in an Open Key
Bobby Johnston — The Saint I Ain't
Jan English Leary — Skating on the Vertical
Julia MacDonnell— The Topography of Hidden Stories
Marjorie Maddox — What She Was Saying
William Marquess — Badtime Stories
William Marquess — Because Because Because Because Because
William Marquess — Boom-shacka-lacka
William Marquess — Things I Want You to Do
Gary Miller — Museum of the Americas
Jennifer Anne Moses — Visiting Hours
Charles Opara — How Hamisu Survived Bad Kidneys and a Bad Son-in-Law